THE YETI SOCIETY

THE YETI SOCIETY

Martin Sexton

AEON

First published in 2017 by
Aeon Books Ltd
118 Finchley Road
London NW3 5HT

Copyright © 2017 by Martin Sexton

The right of Martin Sexton to be identified as the author of this work has been asserted in accordance with §§ 77 and 78 of the Copyright Design and Patents Act 1988.

All rights reserved. No part of this publication may be reproduced, stored in a retrieval system, or transmitted, in any form or by any means, electronic, mechanical, photocopying, recording, or otherwise, without the prior written permission of the publisher.

British Library Cataloguing in Publication Data

A C.I.P. for this book is available from the British Library

ISBN-13: 978-1-91159-707-0

Typeset by Medlar Publishing Solutions Pvt Ltd, India

www.aeonbooks.co.uk

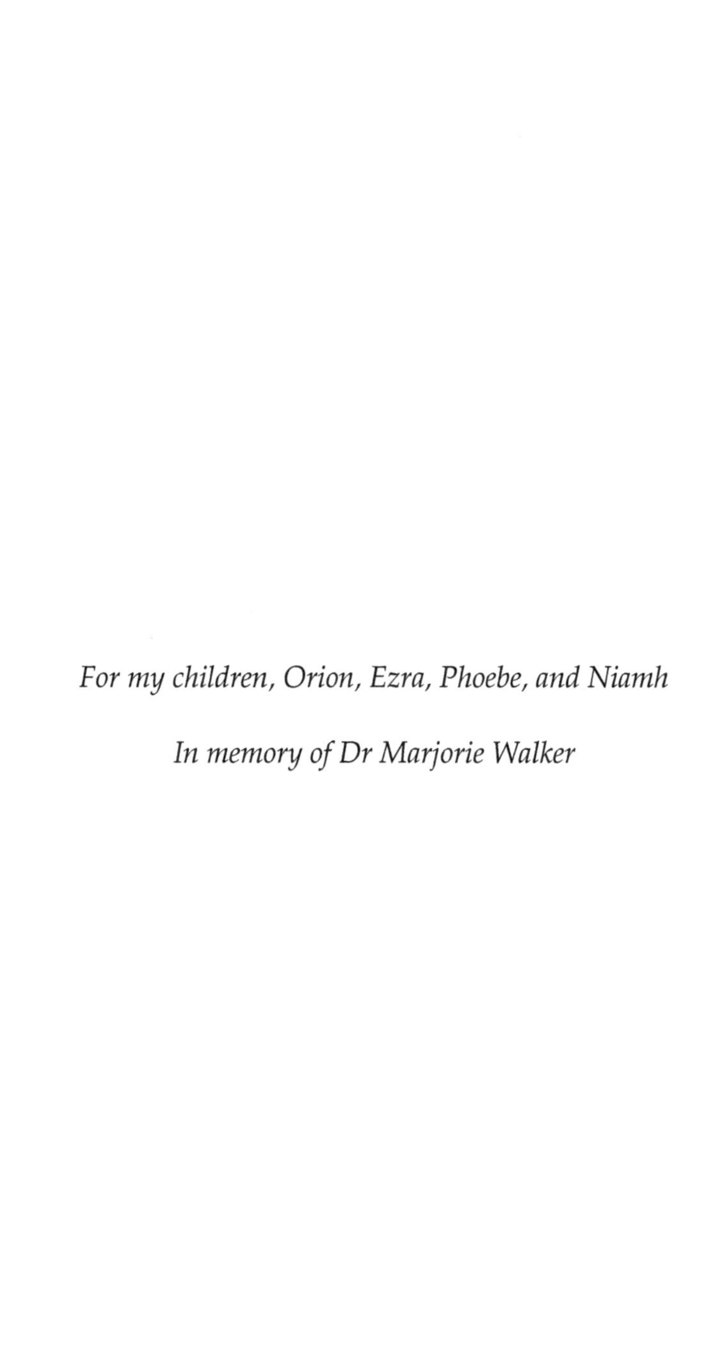

For my children, Orion, Ezra, Phoebe, and Niamh

In memory of Dr Marjorie Walker

CHAPTER ONE

Mohammad went to the Mountain

Mohammad made the people believe he would call a mountain to him, and from the top of it he would offer up his prayers for the observers of his law. So the people assembled; Mohammad called to the Mountain to come to him—again and again, but the Mountain remained still and some of his followers muttered, but he remained unabashed and told his followers to remain patient and then a call came from the Mountain—but only he heard it—it seemed to say to him, 'Come.' So Mohammad stood up and declared he would go, and so he went to the Mountain.

'The Holy Light watches over us.' That is what Mr. Khan would say to me each time he held this old Quran in his hand. Mr. Khan was old, but no one was sure what his real age was. I lived with him in the Hunza in the north-west of Pakistan—the great mountain range was all around us, but few walked this path, only mountain goats and Taliban fighters. But it was another mountain thousands of miles away that was Jabal al Noor or the Holy Light, where the Prophet received his first revelation and this was the reason why Mr. Khan was here and why we had constructed the tunnels and it was why all the Qurans came from far and wide—from places I never knew or had visited. I would carry the old Qurans for Mr. Khan. We would place them inside the great complex of tunnels that ran for over a mile that lay cut into the rock buried beneath the earth like a fox's lair and black as a starless night. Outside was a standing stone the sun had washed white, that was taller than any man and some said was as old as the mountains themselves. Mr. Khan created the tunnels because God had told him so after his visit to the Holy Light in Mecca. In the revelation, he was told the day of judgement was coming and that he, Mr. Khan, must send out word to all the lands of the Prophet and beyond, that all the words of God in the Holy book that had been damaged by accident, fire or through mischief were to be sent to Mr. Khan. If he could he would repair and then make them whole and send them back out to the faithful. Those that were beyond repair he must bury in a mountain till the day of judgement itself.

He had created the tunnels by his own hand at first and everyone said it was a miracle. They had no supports or struts of any kind and one could stand up in them—not just a young boy, but also Mr. Khan, or any of the Taliban fighters that sometimes slept there. Some people would say the tunnels were as the word of God revealed to his Prophet.

Last summer the world shook. A—great earthquake had come and it seemed that it might kill us all. Some of the tunnels collapsed. The Qurans fell off their stacks and were buried. Even every loose sack I helped carefully fill with book after book had been swallowed whole by the Mountain.

But the great stone washed white by the sun remained upright, not even a faint crack was to be found. Mr. Khan said it was God's will and a sign the days were closer to the end because of the wicked and the Kafir and that our work must begin again in earnest as now throughout the lands of the Prophet many Qurans would have been damaged. He sent me out again to the villages—but this time the villagers were angry that I was there to collect broken books and had not offered to help them with anything else. This time they showed no respect and said that the old man was a fool and soon for his grave.

But elsewhere in other places far from the earthquake, other Qurans came, and not long after even the locals forgot their anger, remembered their faith and more books arrived. Sometimes very old Qurans like the one Mr. Khan carries with him arrive. Perhaps 100, 200 or even 400 years old—with beautiful calligraphy and some with the illumination of beautiful patterns and harmonies of wonderful shapes. I often get lost and drift away and study these wonders from the old world.

Most of the books of the Quaran are not so old. If they can be used again, we rebind and then reuse and send them back into the villages and mosques. We only place those that are beyond binding—with fallen loose pages, or those with pages missing, or those with whole parts missing, burnt, stained or torn, with just the fragments of the holy words of God—in the sacks and then place them deep inside the tunnel complex. Sometimes large groups of children my age—some younger, some older—walk on a pilgrimage from the madrasas just to see Mr. Khan's cave of Qurans. I am not sure how many books are here—in whole or part. Mr. Khan says we have 1,000 sacks or more and each full sack I know is itself filled with millions of holy words.

My father told me before he went away to fight with the Mujahideen against the Russians and never came back that he and his father and his father before were descendants of the conquered as well as the followers of the Great King Alexander when he crossed the mountains into Indus. In addition we had the formidable fighting blood of the Khalsa, our ancestors were the initiated Sikhs, but that we also had Mughal relations. He would take me to the odd rock carvings that lay beside the path Alexander's men came by and the world conqueror himself trod. Some carved in Sanskrit left by the Old Kingdom of Tibet when it invaded China and the Indus in the 7th century, but my father said it was much older and that even Alexander saw it. Some of the rocks had giant hairy men and no necks with long extended arms waving, carved into them. One was over two metres high.

The day before he left he sat me and my sister by the rocks and told us of the old world and that where we lived men always fought and this had been the way before even the Holy book and was still the way, but maybe Allah could stop it. He stood up beside the great carved giant and told me that when Alexander crossed into Asia and the Indus, he came across a group of sages who did not bow but stomped their feet by that very rock. One of the sages said to Alexander:

'King Alexander, every man can possess only so much of the earth's surface as this we are standing on and you are mortal like the rest of us, even though you covet and ache for much, much more. You will soon be dead and you will own no more of this earth than that is sufficient to bury your bones.'

Alexander could have killed him on the spot, said my father, but he knew the sage was truly free and spoke the truth and it was then the great Alexander knew he would not return home. My sister and I myself knew our father was talking about himself and we wept. Then our father took our hands and said that we must recite the Throne Verse, as he did, to enter the protection and security of Allah each evening, before we slept or set out on any journey. Then with our final words together, we all recited in unison: 'His throne includeth the heavens and the earth, and He is never weary of preserving them. He is the Sublime, the Tremendous.'

I like old books, old things and manuscripts. My mother and father have a gift for languages. I can put cultured Urdu into good English, I can speak highly colloquial Urdu, Arabic, count in Uzbek, use Punjabi, Braj Bhasha, some Persian, Sanskrit, Brushuski common words. My sister says I also like to swear in English. I went to the Aga Khan middle school and because my father was respected I sometimes stayed in the castle or Baltit Fort in the Hunza Valley by the white-capped mountains. One day my father's teacher let me hold and look at a manuscript that he said was the oldest in the world and told the most ancient of folk tales, the Jataka Tales. He would recite *The Story of the Great Ape*, how the wisest of men, the first man was once born as a great ape and lived as a recluse amidst the forests of the hidden valleys of the Himalaya.

I have a secret. In the Qurans that are sent—sometimes, old postcards or photographs or drawings fall out, with beautiful pictures of far-flung places. Strange cities, great buildings, people dressed in all manner of clothes, even women with painted faces who show their bodies, animals I have never seen. Some of these I keep and look at when Mr. Khan is sleeping. One day as I was sorting through the books an illustration fell out from the pages between the torn bindings, and I read the half-erased title '...tin in Tibet'. It had a young boy like me with a small white dog. He was on a mountain just like the mountains that we hide the books in. A great beast stood up in it, not a bear, but bigger than the tallest man, full of hair, as tall as the great stone outside the cave and like the rock carvings my father showed me. I examined the illustrated mountains and looked again at the strange animal and then gazed hard into the high mountain range all about me and wondered could such a beast live here? It excited me and I became more certain every day that indeed it did. The mountain was not named in these two loose pages but I could just barely read the torn and fuzzy worn type that it was in a place called Tibet and that the boy was called Tin and if the boy Tin could go, so could I. My English was good. I knew this place existed as my father allowed my sister and I to pore over the English atlas our mother had hidden. I knew that the mountains here and about met, and these mountains were linked by valleys and plains and other ranges that made the roof of the world—linking India, Nepal, China, Pakistan, Afghanistan, Bhutan and Tibet. My father was a good fighter and joined the Mujahideen fighting the Russians. He was promised new weapons and money for our family by an American who said as tribal leader if he brought some of the other good fighters along, we would no longer be poor. My father said we were all descended from the great fighters of Huzan who were descendants of the men who followed Alexander the Great. His campaign historian recorded that he saw a tribe of such beings as those carved on the great stones once from his ships, as they navigated into a long river into the Indus and that his men shot arrows at them and Alexander ordered his men to swim to them and catch one but they all fled into the trees; that he had even asked the locals to bring one to him, but they said they could not be caught like other animals. All this would play over and over in my mind. I became lost in this more than anything else each time I gazed at these two faded pages of '…tin in Tibet'.

One morning I awoke determined. I decided that I would go to the mountains. I would leave the old man and the caves and head higher into the range. I would even join the fighters and help them carry their guns and packs if need be; just so I could in turn leave them and find this hairy man of the mountains and the lost tribe Alexander the Great spoke of. Maybe I would find my father too. I, Mohammed, would find the Yeti and do all this and one day they would tell stories of me.

CHAPTER TWO

The Story of the Great Ape

The Universal Soul exists in every individual,
it expresses itself in every creature,
everything in the world is a projection of it.
—The Shevetashvatara Upanishad

The Story of the Great Ape, how the wisest of men, the first Buddha, was once born as a great ape and lived as a recluse in the Himalayan forest. He did not look like nor was he like other monkeys, nor did he behave as such. He was kind and virtuous. A time later, a shepherd got lost following his goats into the mountains and reached the secret forest in the hidden valley. He was exhausted and hungry and climbed to the top of a tree to rest and be safe from the tiger that roamed these mountains. From his vantage point he spied the answer to his appetite, a fruit-rich tree. He moved very carefully, almost like a slow monkey, through the great canopy of the forest towards the fruit tree. Coming closer, the chatter of the birds, insects and other animals of the forest fused with the sound of the great river that carved through the valley. Eventually, he was at the tree and when he reached a branch laden with fruit to pluck them, his eyes were bigger than his belly. He took more than he needed for his fair appetite or for his good balance. What's more, he had overlooked the roots of the tree, which had grown out of a sloping cliff over a waterfall. The branch he held with his free hand, sustaining a good part of his weight, gave way. He lost the fruit and none fell into the pit of the crevice where he lay. He was sore but no bones were broken and he was still hungry. It would make no difference to try again as where he had ended up was deep with sheer hard earth and rock walls and no exit seemed possible. He cursed his goats. Then when he looked up, to his annoyance, one of them stared down at him. It was the longest time he had ever looked directly into the face of one of his goats. Even when he had held a ram down forcibly to castrate it, or kill one for meat, he never really looked at his animals or considered them in any way other than as a means to an end. He knew what a goat looked like, of course, but today he seemed to see it for the first time, for he saw much he had never ever noticed before—that the goat did not have a round black centre in its eye, but a horizontal solid black line as a pupil. This goat stared at him for so long that it left him pondering, was it just these goats or did they all look like that? Then he wondered why did his male and female goats both have beards? He had never ever really considered his goats worth looking at, but rather more looking for, if he lost them. Goats after all, he reasoned, would become feral and return to the wild at the first opportunity. He cursed his goat to get him out of his predicament, for he did know goats were as good at getting out of things as getting into them, having once found several of his goats bleating from the top canopy of a very tall tree. But at this, the goat was gone.

It was then he remembered that he was chastised by an old woman who told him not to beat his goats so harshly, that the goat was a Vahana, a vehicle of the gods. A black goat, ridden by Kali. This was her realm. He would never have a wife or *siddhi* (special powers) granted, as the female Shaiva that follow Kali would know, and curse him back tenfold. The shepherd began to feel sorry for himself but still managed to be angry at his goats.

Then he smelt something, not unlike the stench of a he-goat, but this was a far more powerful odour. Then to his amazement he saw a creature, a Great Ape, but not simply an overgrown monkey. It was large, it stood upright, covered in hair, apart from its face, and was taller, more robust than any man he had ever seen. When the Great Ape saw the distress of the man and his predicament he decided, against his better judgement, to free the man. With difficulty, as the pit was deep, he managed with arduous exertions to rescue him.

The Great Ape ingeniously fashioned a stretcher from two large branches and smaller ones that he elegantly weaved and he hauled the man out and rolled him to the side of the rock fall. The next part was only marginally less difficult than the first—not for the Great Ape alone—but as he was carrying the man, who would have most surely failed by his own effort, even if he had fallen just to the precipice before the rock pit. Finally the man was in a place where he could eventually make his way back to the village. Dusk fell and the Great Ape was exhausted and wished to rest. He motioned to the man to sit beside him and clearly signed that he take first watch and warn him of any tiger in the night and wake him from his rest—for as long as he was not surprised whilst sleeping, he could guard the man against the tiger.

But the man was still frightened and disturbed by the size and strangeness of the beast. He was ungrateful and wished not to remain vulnerable on the ground at night and to hide high in the tree canopy until dawn. His heart was hardened and he remained resentful despite his rescue. He decided he would take his chances on his own, without the Ape. A panic and darkness entered him and at once he decided he would kill the sleeping Great Ape. He found a large heavy stone and held it swaying above him to let it drop silently and crush the skull of the beast, but his cowardice skewed his aim and the weight of the stone slipped and merely grazed the Great Ape. It was a little dazed and struggled more from the deep slumber of its sleep than the blow, but it was more hurt by what the man had done. The Great Ape held the man fast and gave him a liquefying stare, of anger and pity. Unlike the goat, the Great Ape's gaze flashed the entire animal kingdom as a prism from the crystal sapphire blue and whirlpool black centre of its eyes—it happened like a lightning flash—it was far too overwhelming for the man to contemplate. The shepherd shook in terror and broke out in a sweat of guilt from every pore.

The Great Ape released him and it spoke to him for the very first time:

> Brought back from the mouth of Death
> When you reached the other world.
> Saved from one precipice
> Thou has now fallen into another
> Upon what ignorance is man driven to such vices and cruelties and chooses to bathe in such miseries.
> The delusions you fixate that fall on the false hope of a misguided prosperity.
> The pain of this blow does not aggrieve me as much
> As the thought that on account of me
> You have struck it
> and plunged yourself into greater evil
> From where I or no one else can rescue thee.

Nonetheless, the Great Ape did not kill the man; in its compassion and mercy it escorted the man to the edge of the forest so he could return to his fellow beings.

Time went on: the man suffered, he neither washed nor bathed nor cut his hair or nails. His goats that had remained chose to humiliate him. They no longer went feral and broke into his home and slept there. He became so miserable that he was shunned and expelled from society.

Excommunicated he ran from his world and back to the dense forest, where what remained of his dishevelled clothes dissolved. Naked, he skulked in the forest and hid from any disturbance, but still a coward, he clung to his life and barely slept, remaining fearful each night that a tiger may slay and eat him. One day a retinue of the king's hunters came across him in the forest hunting. Thinking they had found a strange beast, they wounded him and brought him before the king, who had camped nearby. Shocked, both he and his entourage thought they had been brought a strange monkey, until the naked, broken man spoke. Fatally wounded and near to death, the unrecognisable goat herder finally found the courage to repent and speak in the hope that, in his remaining breath, he might find some peace and redeem his soul. The king listened, astonished at his sorrowful tale, and was so moved he ordered the hunt to cease. He declared the forest and mountains a sacred sanctuary to the supreme mystery, to all its gods, to the wise and compassionate Great Ape and all that lived in its range. For any tree that was cut down, he ordered a strict sanction that ten must be planted in its place. He sent out a decree that large stones be set around its natural boundaries of rivers and plains and any and all trails that led to it, and that on the rocks should be carved images of the Great Ape. He did this so no man in the future could excuse himself of ignorance and insult this intermediary of the gods and thus defile this place again.

CHAPTER THREE

Eve at Bluff Creek

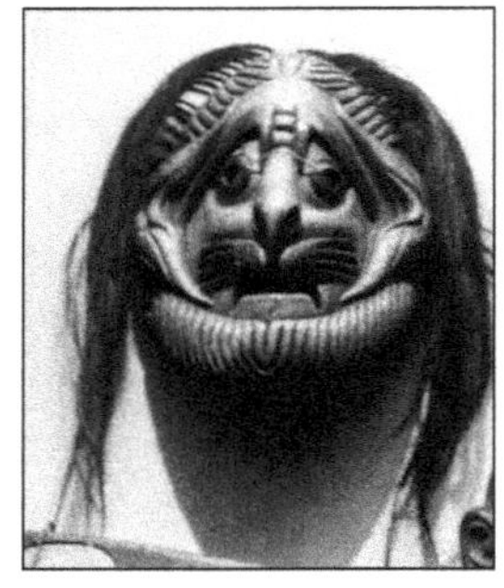

> Bigfoot is real. Absolutely breathes, eats, mates, lives, and they are our brothers and sisters, they are not animals, they are human beings with a soul, just as all humans have.
>
> —Red Elk, of the Blackfoot and Shoshoni Nations

'Bigfoot is the white man's name, the locals call it See'atko, Skookum, Oh Mah, Sasquatch—but there are as many names for it as there are indigenous tribes of our ancient lands they call North America and these names have been here as long as we have had stories to tell of them, a thousand years and more before the invaders came. That's what Snowstorm, medicine woman of the Karuk peoples told me and I can tell you, if it is a hoax, it is a hoax like no other, and if it is real, it changes everything; either way it is beautiful, real or not.'

That is what Ross said each time he spoke of the scratchy faded colour film. He was a scientist and as rational as they come. He declared himself a sceptic, a believer in nothing. Ross did not even believe his own eyes, having seen an animal up by a creek on the Kalmuth River. It stood up, its back to him, then stepped—he said he thought he saw it take at least one to two steps forward—then it was down on all fours into the woods, disappeared from sight almost immediately. It looked odd, but he then managed to convince himself later it was a bear. But he knew being alone in the woods, amongst bear, coyote, mountain lion and deer, the sound of owls and unidentified bird call, one could easily listen too much to one's own power of suggestion. Sometimes things looked odd in the wilderness. People themselves also became odd, alone in such wild places. Even though Ross was a sceptic he talked endlessly of this film.

The film baffled him. I had never seen it, only heard him talk of it. Though a scientist, he would talk of it like a disciple would of a religious event, a miracle.

One day we heard something at a high elevation, a powerful ape-like whoop, up above the treeline in the high mountain, then a crashing through, into the woods below. The ground shook under the great weight of this something that seemed to be walking on feet, not hoofs or pads and claws, but heavy steps separated out in what seemed like giant strides down a precipitous side of the mountain. Yet we saw nothing. We had only the long list of all that was actually real in the forest and on the mountain, that we turned over and over again in our minds and in our conversation, in order to stop our imaginations running riot. I knew that once we got back to the cabin, I would go to the town and see the film that Ross kept talking about. Shot in 1967 here in Bluff Creek, just 20 miles from where we heard the commotion and where we slept uneasily that night. As we drove back down the old logging road in the truck, the radio was playing the song 'A Girl Like You'.

Ross's cousin Ruth lived in the town and had an old projector that she used to show Bible Class films to the children at the local church. At real expense, Ross had managed to obtain a print of the original stock film and he said it would be the first thing we did once we hit town.

Ruth was an attractive, middle-aged woman. Even though she was five years older than me, she had this innocent look about her. She wore no make-up and was confident in her skin. She was a Southern Baptist who had not shaken her religious upbringing. To find the film, we had to go through boxes of Bibles, books on theology and numerous old prints of religious events from the Old and New Testaments. Those not in boxes or in piles on the floor were on the walls in frames or pinned or in rolls on the mantelpiece. I saw the furniture of Ruth's mind before I met Ruth. And if there was any doubt, we had arrived early evening and Eric said she would be out at church.

Every picture on her wall was religious—but with mountains. Jesus and the Sermon on the Mount, Jesus in the desert mountains casting down Satan, Moses getting the tablets on Mount Sinai, Moses seeing the Burning Bush on the sacred Bedouin Mountain—then one that missed my Sunday school education—Ross had to explain it was Aaron being buried or taken up on a mountain in Jordan. He told me, even though, like me, he did not believe in God, that it was best to be respectful to Ruth, not just because we were guests that evening, but because she had been through a lot and this was how she dealt with it.

I was drawn to a particular picture, a print of an etching. It depicted a vast Jordanian desert down to the Red Sea with large mountains all around. Moses stood before his priest—a horizontal Aaron, with his hands held up to the sky, rays emerging from broken clouds. For some reason the picture gave me a feeling of vertigo, a feeling that had strangely escaped me from the real mountains we had just left, but was unexpectedly and dizzily present on this imagined range.

Grouped together, I was struck by how many apocryphal religious events happen in mountains. My mind returned to what we had heard and felt the night before. I was suddenly reminded and excited to see Ross' film. The controversial 1967 short film, the Patterson-Gimlin film. A cowboy, Bob Gimlin and an adventurer and self-confessed Bigfoot hunter, Roger Patterson, went looking for the beast of the woods and mountains, an unlikely search for what the local tribes call Oh Mah or Sasquatch, the boss of the mountains and then … they found him.

Except the him was a her. It was clearly a female, all hair and mammary glands. Its breasts, along with its heavily muscled thighs, moved with gravity and an hallucinatory clarity through the very few seconds of the shaken film amongst the flood damage of the Klamath River in Bluff Creek. The beast was not hidden, obscured by vegetation, a notorious blob Squatch. It was in plain sight, on a clear sun-drenched afternoon. One had one simple conclusion to draw—either it was a very large man in an ape-like suit or it was real. It was a binary choice. There was no in-between.

I lost count of how many times we screened that film, over and over again that night. We watched, largely silent, our only words being, occasionally … Shall we look at it again? One more time, yes? And so we did … Again and again. It looked strange. My eyes were at war with my brain and then vice versa as both would jump from opposing conclusions. The repeated screenings did not help matters, one set of eyeballs convinced one it was real and another viewing did not add clarity but left the same set rejecting the previous conviction. Eric was right, if it was a hoax it was a work of genius and if it was real … well …

Then Ruth walked in. We were so engrossed we did not hear her, even though the film is entirely silent. She switched the lights on and the first words I heard her say were, 'You watching Eve again, Ross?' I stood up to clumsily greet her but she ignored me and walked to the kitchen. She continued, 'That's naked Eve. God sent her to show us we have to begin again. Judgement day is coming. Who's your friend? I have only got basics from the store, if you want eating.'

The next morning I set about finding out as much as I could on the background of the Bluff Creek film, of the strange hairy bipedal figure that had Ross and myself second guessing every time we watched it. His obsession had infected me. Unknowingly I found myself entering a world of clashing European empires and the mountains of the word. Nearly two decades before the Bluff Creek film, I found out that a world away, on the Nepalese side of the vast Himalaya, two highly respected English mountaineers had discovered inexplicable tracks. Eric Shipton along with a Dr Michael Ward were shocked on their descent down the Melung Chu, unroped but still on a dangerous uncharted climb close together, to find on a desolate glacier at an elevation of 16,000ft a long trackway in virgin snow. Despite the snow combined with hardened ice, deep depressions of large and bare, unadorned bipedal hominoid footprints were in a long run. As they were the first humans to chart this unexplored area, and at such an altitude to find anything, any animal was uncanny. They pondered could it be another climber? But surely only correctly equipped mountaineers with appropriate footwear, indeed any footwear would have made some sense. Truly baffled they took some photographs of what they found. Having no means to accurately measure the individual footprints, Shipton took what would become two iconic photographs that would stun and shock the world. One with Ward's boot for scale beside it and, the most iconic of all, one with Ward's ice axe beside it. What is more, two other equally respected mountaineers on the same expedition, including a scientist, Bourdillon, had followed them a day later over the Menlung La and come across the same trackway. Equally baffled, they followed it for over 3 miles before they had to turn back. When they returned to the high elevation base camp they met with the highly respected and experienced Sherpa Sen Tensing (who would later, along with Edmund Hillary, be the first to reach the summit of Everest). His local knowledge, having been raised and lived near and on the mountains, gave him no doubt. He confirmed they were footprints of a Yeti. The extraordinary photographs and the back story of how they came across them began in 1951 when Ward, a doctor with the Royal Army Medical Corps, came across some hidden photographs of the unexplored Nepalese south side of Everest taken by an RAF Mosquito X1X. The photographs revealed some key features critical to any ascent of the highest mountain in the world from the Nepalese side.

Two years earlier all foreigners were barred from entering Nepal and all Everest expeditions had to take place from the Tibet side. Along with these critical aerial photographs, he unearthed a rare and forgotten photogrammetric survey from the 1930s. Ward felt he had found the means for a successful ascent of Everest from Nepal. His attempts at getting such an ascent going with help from the Royal Geographical Society and the Alpine Club proved difficult, not least because his plan meant a crossing of the treacherous Khumbu Icefalls and its maze of cliffs and shifting deadly crevasses. Ward managed to convince two New Zealanders, including Hillary, to join him along with Englishman Eric Shipton. When they finally arrived in Nepal and climbed the 18,000ft to the icefall, Ward described it as,

'... a glimpse into purgatory, the icefall had become an immense, unstable ruin, as though an earthquake had shaken the entire glacier.'

Nepal lies on a major fault-line between two tectonic plates. One has the continent of India resting upon it and pushes east and north at a rate of 2cm a year against the other, which carries Asia and Europe: it is the very process that created the vast Himalaya mountain range.

It was this expedition, and towards its end, as they were exploring the south-west of Everest in the Gauri Sankar at an elevation of 16,000ft on the glacier of the Mending basin, that Eric Shipton and Dr Ward found the tracks. Sherpa guide Sen Tensing had no doubt that what they first saw and photographed was a Yeti. At this altitude and in such a remote place on earth, the prints were fresh, they could only have been made that day or the night before, possibly very late the previous day. Shipton and Ward followed the tracks for a mile but the heavy loads they were carrying and the altitude and the pressing reminder as to what was their actual task, researching an ascent of Everest, caused them reluctantly to abandon the tracking. I found that many other respected mountaineers, both before and since Shiptons's photographs, had seen footprints at impossible elevations. As far back as 1925 the geologist N.A. Tombazi witnessed a naked, hairy man at a distance in Tibet, on the Himalaya, and went to investigate the area. He saw the clear bipedal prints left behind. Tombazi, the leader of the 1925 British Geological Expedition, was convinced he had witnessed a Yeti.

He saw it, spoke about it and then wrote about it. They all thought he was mistaken, but Reinhold Messner thought, 'I know the high mountains and I can name every animal on the mountain, and in the valleys below and the great high plateaus.' And just maybe Messner could. After all, Reinhold Messner had climbed Everest. He was a great mountaineer, maybe the greatest. Reinhold with his partner Peter Habeler had been the first to ascend to the very top of Everest without supplemental oxygen. Indeed, Messner had conquered all the highest mountains on earth, fourteen of them, and all over 26,000ft without supplemental oxygen and frequently on his own for the greater part of the final ascent. But this was what his detractors used against him. Mountain men are competitive and could not stand Reinhold's success or, worse, the attention it got him. So they said he was mistaken. All that climbing without supplemental oxygen had given him anoxia or brain damage and made him unreliable. Not only had a lack of oxygen damaged his cognitive functions, but bizarrely and conversely, he had compensated by sucking up all the oxygen of publicity for their achievements and if that was not enough, he wanted more of the spotlight for his ridiculous claims. The criticism was sharp and was designed to unnerve him. Reinhold was not just disliked for his success, for many years before he was equally and more devastatingly loathed for his perceived failures.

A personal tragedy took place on a mountain, one which directly hurt him and his family, so it was even stranger that the death of his younger brother led to him being despised in his grief for something that had a lesser impact on others.

If Reinhold thought he could finally leave his detractors behind him atop the highest mountains in the world, on isolated peaks away from civilisation, he was wrong. The death of his closest brother Gunther happened in 1970. Following and during a dangerous ascent, an even more hazardous descent took place down the Himalayan peak of the Naked Mountain or Nanga Parbat, as it sloped down deep snow, avalanche, sheer ice walls and unforgiving scree into the foothills of the beautiful valley of Gilgit Pakistan below. This death of his brother was to follow him every day, a shadow of spectral density that served to drive him, but one which his enemies fed on like hungry ghosts. Fourteen years after Reinhold lost his brother on the descent down the mountain, Werner Herzog (the German filmmaker) found out Messner was returning to climb—not the Naked Mountain itself, as it had taken eight of his ten toes, but a less dangerous climb of the mountains nearby. Herzog asked Messner at the base camp, 4000ft up, the night before the ascent: 'Do you suppose you two brothers were so close, your brother died in your place, and may have given you a different attitude towards death?'

Messner replied, 'I have a different attitude towards death in general because of climbing and perhaps because of my brother's death. Even though I still have the feeling he is alive, and not just in dreams, but say when I look at the mountains we climbed together. We were together in the hardest climb I have ever been on, we were in the tough situations and one was responsible for the other if we fell, and that welded us together so intensely that we can never be separated again. And whenever I look at that rock face today … I have the feeling he is still alive and I feel those hard, dangerous, so intense moments again, just as he feels them as if he were with me. I don't have that feeling he died in my place. I have the feeling that I myself died in that expedition.'

Although Messner was used to controversy in as much as anyone could be, the insults he received around the death of his brother were even harder to take, as they not only came from those whom he set out with on that fatal day but these same fellow climbers formed the small group that both he and his brother always looked for some support from. Reinhold and Gunther were brothers but something even deeper bound them. Their father Joseph was a World War I veteran, who returned to the small alpine village in the Villnoss Valley, shell-shocked, unable to come to terms with his war fatigue or to safely process his violent rages either against the dogs they kept, his nine children, or their long-suffering mother. One day Reinhold went looking for his younger brother Gunther and found him, after much searching, cowering in the dog kennel. Their father had beaten him so badly with the dog whip he was unable to walk. He helped him and tried to protect him from his father's later rages. Reinhold learnt to stand up to his father so by the age of 10 his beatings were not as severe. Together they shared this terrible secret about their father whom they also tried to love, but Gunther and Reinhold had also become wise children and bonded allies against the injustices of the world.

As they grew up, young Reinhold and Gunther impressed the older, more established climbers and were invited on what would turn out to be this most fatal climb in 1969/70.

Neither Gunther nor Reinhold knew that this climb was organised because of an obsession by the team leader regarding his half-brother Willy Merkl who had led a fatal expedition financed by Nazi Germany in 1934 and the particular Nazi fantasy around all things mountainous and epic. An attempt in 1932 by Merkl had failed, as he was hopelessly unprepared for the challenges of the Himalaya. This time, despite Nazi funding and to add to the delusion, Merkl had wanted the entire team, including two other climbers and six sherpas, to immediately arrive at the summit in a grand finale fitting of a Leni Riefenstahl film starring or directed by her. Riefenstahl happened to be a favourite of Hitler, as indeed were all 'Bergfilme' or mountain films produced under the rise of the Nazis. This time Merkl was one of many German climbers who wished to turn fantasy into fact. His mob-handed ascent proved fatal when all the climbers and the sherpas died. In 1938, another German expedition found his frozen body, along with a sherpa, in a snow cave. The 1932 and the 1938 teams were members of the German and Austrian Alpine Club, both nationalistic and rife with anti-Semitism and with a notorious 'Aryan paragraph' going back as far as 1899 in its club documents.

In the same year as the new Nazi-funded expedition found its dead predecessors in 1938 and brought the bodies down wrapped in the swastika flag, the German and Austrian Alpine Club was given a new name, Deutscher Alpenverein (DAV), under the new leadership of Arthur Seyss-Inquart, an unwavering anti-Semite, devoted Nazi and war criminal. Eight years later Seyss-Inquart would be hanged at the Nuremberg Trials. The Nazi darling of film, Leni Riefenstahl, maker of pan-Germanic mountain films, who would be feted and photographed relaxing with Hitler, Goebbels and Himmler, would go on to direct the disturbing dark propaganda masterpieces, 'Will to Power' and 'Olympia' for the Third Reich. She escaped a Nuremberg trial but was ostracised by the intellectuals and cultured artists whom she had claimed to be part of, having her last film banned entry into the Cannes Film Festival in 1954. She spent the post-war years obsessed by more aggrandised colonial body gawking—this time of the Nubia. She ended up reduced to skimming along the bottom of the dimmer fashion world, who would continue to admire her body fetish films as harbingers of the empty consumerist and selfie, looks-obsessed future and its constructed false narratives that awaited—which are her later photography and films' only true legacy.

Both Seyss-Inquart and Riefenstahl stood in stark contrast to two other mountain climbers and more modest and truly cultured fellow German speakers, who also both happened to be associates of the German and Austrian Alpine Club (subsequently excluded due to their non-Aryan status). One was Viktor Frankl, who despite being kicked out, formed his own mountaineering club with fellow Jews. This highly respected therapist, physician and pioneering psychiatrist was deported from Vienna into a Nazi ghetto in 1942. Then, in 1944, he was transported to Auschwitz with his wife. They became separated and she was finally state-murdered after being moved again to Bergen-Belsen. Viktor Frankl was then transported to a slave camp, where he worked for 5 months close to Dachau, and moved to yet another camp associated with Dachau before he was finally liberated in April 1945. Despite this, Viktor Frankl survived and helped others who had survived and contemplated suicide at the bleakness of the world by his Logotherapy process.

Another mountaineer, Fred Zinnemann, was also a film-maker. In 1929, he helped shoot 'People on a Sunday' in Berlin. He managed to see the signs and escaped later that year to America. Unlike Riefenstahl, Zinnemann's films received 65 Oscar nominations, winning 24, and included 'High Noon' and 'From Here to Eternity'. His last film was shot in the Alps, where he used to hike and climb as a young man, and where Reinhold and Gunther set out.

Reinhold ran to and climbed to danger, as did his brother Gunther. Reinhold was excited to do the climb not just because this was a truly grand mountain but also because one of his childhood climbing heroes, Hermann Buhl, had managed to be the first man to get to its summit in 1953 without supplemental oxygen. It had claimed 31 lives by the time Hermann Buhl had pushed his luck and reached its top but he was even luckier to have made it down alive. On the slow descent, the light was dimming fast and he had to stand upright on a tiny ledge with an 8000ft fall for an entire night before the dawn light could help him navigate a safe way down. The southern face of the mountain had not been attempted and was considered suicidal, even by Buhl, but this would be the first that Messner and this new team would attempt, scaling the unforgiving sheer rock of the southern Rupal Face. It was here he lost his brother Gunther:

'I made my first Himalayan expedition in 1970 and we reached the summit of Nanga Parbat in two roped teams. Of the four of us, I am the only one still alive. My brother died on Nanga Parbat. In 1972, I climbed Manaslu in Nepal, the 7th highest in the world. One of the members of the team froze to death on a small plateau just beneath the summit. Another went mad and died. In all those years I would meet mountaineers, mostly Englishmen, the best in the world, then I would learn later they were dead, killed on the mountains.'

Maybe Reinhold should have seen that even his hero Hermann Buhl was not infallible. The mountains were unforgiving. Just a few years after his conquest of Nanga Parbat, bravery and stamina and luck combined and he reached the summit of Broad Peak, again in the vast range of the Himalaya where the mountains infiltrate Pakistan and Kashmir. But attempting its neighbouring mountain, Chogolisa, he stepped out over a ledge in a snowstorm, triggering an avalanche. His body has never been recovered and remains entombed in the ice. But Reinhold Messner ignored all of that and chose to make this fatal climb.

In his body Reinhold was walking, but in his mind he was in a loop of the death dance of all the tragedies that had beset him. In this Messner may have supposed he was no different to anyone else of his fellow climbers, walking and climbing to stop his constant internal dialogue.

On one such walk in the mountains the voice inside his head had indeed dissolved and he began to once more attune to the sounds outside. But something this time was very different: first he felt an unsettling presence, and then he heard something very large, very close, and as the dusk was setting its dimming switch all around, he saw it. He saw a beast, but not a snow leopard or a monkey or a bear, he saw this something, but what was it? He started to tread more carefully up the steep slope full of obscuring vegetation and trees to get a better look. The something moved very fast, making light work of the obstacles of nature all around, almost gliding between the trees. It was upright. It could not be a bear, could it? It was fifty metres away, he surmised. He moved towards it very slowly, trying to hold his breath and calm himself, as his beating heart added an internal sound that he was worried could be audible. The pulsing of his blood gave him the same nervous excitement he felt on a steep precipice or a moving icefall opening up to a deep yawning crevasse. He was close, maybe too close, as he suddenly felt hot adrenaline, not just inside him, but also concretely in front of him, for here stood upright real hair and real blood to match his—just metres away—as the beast stopped too suddenly and turned back to face him in the dim light. It had short legs, supporting an odd torso and over-long arms, covered in matted hair. Then it seemed to spit or hiss at him as a warning: this far and no further. He glimpsed a flash of teeth and eyes. Then, to Reinhold's relief, it moved away and at great speed, but not before he could clearly see its tracks, bipedal and like what exactly? Its footprints told Messner it was no phantom.

He collected himself, but then a great fear entered him. He was alone and what little light there was had almost turned to moonlight. He had lost the village he was looking for, and was at 13,000ft or 14,000ft elevation. The river he had crossed earlier was deeper, and the current stronger, than he had surmised. He could now feel the cold chill further up from his wet feet that had not quite dried from the walking. How far had he walked? Where was he? In his mind a memory arose from his past and stood fast in front of him. His parents, Josef and Maria, had taken him and his elder brother Helmut on an alpine climb, but it was more fittingly a hike than a walk. With Helmut aged six and Reinhold just three, they became tired and protested about going any further. His mother then said, 'You two wait here by this tree, we will walk on a while.' Reinhold heard his brother Helmut crying. Reinhold asked Helmut, 'Do you know the way home, if mama and papa don't come back?' Reinhold was not sure if he was whispering this out loud, but then he heard Helmut say inside his head, 'No.' This memory so long ago buried was intrusive and unwelcome. But a thousand and more miles away, a long deceased brother away, his heart was still pounding, he could hear clearly, as it was resonating and amplified by the tree he was hiding behind. Pump,

pump, pulsed his blood into his body and head as he became one with and it seemed morphed into the tree he hid beside. Reinhold stood like this for a while, he was not sure how long, but long enough until the memory of first his parents, than Helmut, faded and the sensation stopped. He suddenly found his boldness and his logic once more, 'This is bullshit, what am I doing? Who am I? I am Reinhold Messner, I am Messner.' He said this several times out loud to reassure himself. This something kept crashing into his mind, it was wild and it was large, seven feet tall, with strength and maybe intelligence as well? He tried to remember Gunther and all the things that drove him and to collect himself and vanquish his fear. He decided to hunt this beast down and see that it was a bear. After all that's all it could surely be?

He would spend 12 more years searching for it in another obsession that had him entering a correspondence with Ernst Schaefer regarding the possible existence of the Yeti. But nothing happened again and doubts entered—or was it something else? He stood back from his original claim. But Messner was a better mountaineer, a better man. The Sherpas, even though they thought he was odd, respected him, they saw he was different. But was the truth behind Messner stepping back, the real absolute truth, because he wanted to protect this amazing unique beast? He had written to the controversial Ernst Schaefer, whose SS sponsored and Nazi supported Tibet trip of 1938–39 ended in Schaefer being told by the Sherpas that a Yeti was living in a cave. So he went and found the nearest cave and shot a large, rare Tibetan blue bear, that could offer no resistance as it was hibernating.

In an earlier expedition in 1916, another team member, Hugo Weigold, had been the first westerner to witness a giant panda in the wild and he had attempted to bring a panda cub back—which he obtained by most likely killing or scaring off the mother. The cub subsequently died. This was not a good start to interspecies relations and western mountain men.

When Reinhold went back to look for his dead brother and attempt a climb at Nanga Parbat, he witnessed an echo of the Nazi mob assault led by Merkl back in 1932. This time a group of itinerant climbers waiting to go up was so large that Reinhold's usual enthusiasm to climb dissipated and for the very first time he turned back and went home. The recent phenomenon of the 'tourist route' up Mount Everest was perhaps another reason behind Messner changing his mind from seeing a Yeti to seeing a bear (for he was adamant at first it was no bear). The truth is that as far back as 1953 the British had created the largest circus in order to 'conquer' Everest with what could be best described as a small invading army of 365 people. This included 350 porters and Sherpas, eleven British mountaineers, and two New Zealanders, with one Tibetan and one Nepalese these being 'semi-official' climbers.

Even in a remote place like the Himalaya, Ernst Schaefer was murdering rare bears and Weigold abducting endangered pandas in 1916, and 365 people were arriving all at once in 1953 to get one of the British men to Everest's summit. In the end it was not a Brit but a New Zealand man and a Tibet/Nepalese guide who got there, despite the nationalist Union Jack claims in England. There was some karmic justice that a modest bee-keeping Kiwi and an equally modest hard-working indigenous guide were the first to make it to the summit of the Great Mother.

Eric Shipton was excluded from this expedition, partly because he sensed its aggrandised 'colonial empire' scale was idiotic and as far removed from him and his small team (including Hillary) who had opened the route to a successful ascent in the first place. He was honest when he and Ward found the Yeti tracks two years before and he was succinct when he wrote to the Joint Himalayan Committee formed of the Alpine Club and the Royal Geographical Society (where he would have been the natural choice to attempt this well-financed venture, as he had successfully led the Mount Everest reconnaissance expedition in Nepal in 1951). As Shipton stated to them, 'My well-known dislike of large expeditions and my abhorrence of a competitive element in mountaineering might well seem out of place in the current situation.' It sealed his fate and he was excluded despite the protests from a loyal, decent Hillary who risked his own exclusion by protesting directly to the British Army Colonel John Hunt, later Lord Hunt, who led the expedition.

To recent date there have been over 7000 such ascents to its summit at an average cost of the princely sum of $65,000 as the price of entry for each climber, and bottled oxygen at every point up the mountain with fixed ropes put in place by 'high altitude workers' who also carry tents and other equipment and food supplies, and standard helicopter insurance required for each and every climber. What chance had the Yeti of being left alone or surviving as a rare species if scientifically confirmed to be 'real?'

Messner woke from a nightmare once. They had not only installed a fast elevator to the summit of Everest but a leisurely escalator down.

Despite my crash-course, I realised I knew very little, if anything, about Tibet and yet I told Ross of my findings. He laughed but he also looked shell-shocked, like a fellow addict in a meeting. He had, or the film, or the mountains, or Bluff Creek or these bona fide witnesses had, infected me with their captivating stories in remote places and tantalising evidence, but of what exactly?

I remembered seeing the Frank Capra movie 'Lost Horizon', based on the 1933 novel by James Hilton, as a child. Its construction of the temples of Tibet and the mythical kingdom of Shangri-La were beautiful and exquisite but wholly false Hollywood sets, yet in their handmade craft they surpassed artificial contemporary computer-generated images. They were fabricated as interiors far from the East off a busy Los Angeles highway. The exteriors representing the Himalaya were shot in the Mojave Desert, Palm Springs and the Sierra Nevada Mountains. Just like the preternatural female Sasquatch in the 1967 film at Bluff Creek, they had the uncanny about them, real theatre and magic.

Bluff Creek and the valleys and forests and mountains and Six Rivers national forest were just a hike away, but it was suddenly not enough. I had to devour all I could on Tibet and the Himalaya and I shared this all with Ross.

Then Ruth walked in and said, 'If you want to know about Tibet ask a real Tibetan. There's one my daughter sees in Colorado. Personally, I think he's a fake. He looks more like a Charlie, a North Viet Cong commie to me, anyhow, that's a two hour flight or a day's drive. My daughter insists he's the real deal, a monk apparently. He is nothing like a proper Christian priest, mind, but he is a preacher or a teacher, as Jo says. I told her Jesus is your Lord and Saviour, not some monk from Tibet. Jo is wilful since her father's death from alcohol and other issues, but she has his goddamn stubborn streak.'

Ross said Jo was a young kid and, like her mother, had been through a lot, maybe too much, and she was just finding her way in life. He said, 'This ain't Shangri-La like in Lost Horizon, but it is Shambhala, which is the Tibetan origin behind our concept of Shangri-La, or at least that's what the monk calls it, even if it's the Rockies. Jo says that he is what they call a Rinpoche, not just any old monk, that's a respected reincarnated teacher in Buddhism, Ruth.'

Ruth walked back out again, talking back, 'I am driving out in two days to see Jo. Come along if you like, both of you, but I want money for gas. If you fly you book your own ticket but get me one too. Be useful, help me break her free of that commie-Buddhist cult.'

CHAPTER FOUR

Crazy Wisdom

Drive-in Saturday

In Tibet and Bhutan and parts of Nepal, amongst the respected elder teachers or Rinpoches, sometimes a unique holy man appears. Some say such a man can appear in two places at once, that such a man can manufacture objects or phantoms, conjure things, just through pure thought alone. The respected Rinpoches have a name for such a manifestation and for the secret tantric teaching that goes with it.

It was 7th October 1950, the Year of the Tiger, a Saturday and it was turning to night. Chogyam Trungpa even as a boy of eleven years old was a fiercely intelligent and insightful young monk. He enjoyed constantly questioning his tutors, as well as himself. He was having an encounter with the highly revered

Guru Rinpoche, a respected lama from the 7th century—he was not dreaming, just meditating. Earlier that day, and without permission, he had unfurled the large, heavily brocade-framed thangka after invoking, again without permission, the Nechung Oracle, taking out the circular mirror of divination, the Melong, with its sacred mantra, and placed it on his chest. He had wrapped himself with seven layers of clothing, including the final ornate golden silk robe. Heavy for even a healthy adult monk, Chogyam submitted to laying on the floor as he struggled to stand up wearing the 80 pound regalia that crowned the ensemble, along with the harness that held the four flags and three victory banners, all of which was now threatening to nail him to the ground as he struggled on the floor. Laying there he felt a sudden horizontal vertigo, as if he was drowning in the sartorial pool of multiple layers that promised to transport the wearer into the future. Yet Chogyam, as he stared up into the hollow of the stupa, was conversely thinking only of the past. For it was an illustration on an exquisite 16th century thangka roll that had captivated him and he was magnetised by an image of a figure. Unlike the usual deities and multiple demons, saints and monks and lay people, a blue-faced and hairy white bipedal figure, which was oversized in proportion to the mountain which it lay beside, jumped out at him. He had difficulty re-rolling the vast painting and then cramming all the Oracle clothing and its unwieldy equipment back into the impossibly small chest he had pulled it out of. Luckily its location had been revealed to him in a transcendent state, by the deceased Crazy Wisdom master Rinpoche Khenpo Ghanshawr. Quickly he closed the rusted lock he had picked, hiding all evidence in time from his teachers. The excitement of his illicit act, combined with the rush of blood to his head under the weight of the regalia, served to burn even deeper the rendering of the hairy man into his mind. And it was thus that he happened to be contemplating the Yeti or gigantic snowman, or what is known in the west as the Abominable

Snowman. Looking back, Chogyam grew a little confused. Was it then, wearing the heavy Oracle clothing flat on his back, or was it a little later while meditating when the visitor from the past appeared. Regardless, the 7th century time traveller asked Chogyam a question. Would he like to join a secret occult order, The Yeti Society? Chogyam, being Chogyam, argued with his time traveller friend and said that occult orders have long lost the significance that was once attached to them in Guru Rinpoche's time, and at this epoch they have ceased being orders at all and have become merely societies, where all sorts of special aims are pursued; for fostering particular vanities and the like, with internal hierarchies and beset with insufferable egos and trapdoors for even the initiated to fall through.

They are merely societies, Chogyam said to his transcendent friend. Indeed, he went on, they are no longer repositories for any special knowledge but are constructs of an empty formalism and dead ritual. As he said this, Chogyam was mindful that he may as well be just talking of current Buddhist practice or indeed any variant of religious practice anywhere. He became more strident with the Guru Rinpoche that he held in his mind: 'Today is the age of publicity and it will not tolerate artificial secrecy or artificial mystery. Our age wants everything to come out into the open!' Chogyam declared so loudly that it broke his meditation and his time traveller friend dissolved at the same moment Chogyam's thoughts became words spoken out loud into the empty, shaded colonnade of the temple.

Having startled himself, Chogyam stood up and stared as if he was looking at the walls for the first time, at the faded painted figures with a faint echo of the rolled paintings on the thangka. The four dignitaries who are guardians of the four directions, sat two on either side of the doorway—as they do in all temples across the roof of the world, from Nepal down to the Swat Valley in Pakistan, to the climbing roads of northern India and to the borders of China and beyond all directions of the Himalaya. Yet at that moment, to Chogyam, the kings seemed animated, as if they were boldly staring him down, eight forensic eyeballs, bathing him in a cold acid bath of reason and harsh Himalayan winds from the four compass points they represented. Chogyam became nervous and was thinking he may have bitten off more than he could manage when he consulted the Oracle. Had he contaminated the Five Pure Lights, with the Five Poisons in his ignorance, pride, aversion, attachment, and envy? The red-painted doors were imperial and unforgiving, the great hall was death with silence, all the lamps that should have been illuminating the dark corners in front of the shrines were extinguished and the tail end of their smoke was sucked out of the small open windows set in the high walls. The marble floor was immensely cold on his bare feet. He looked up and in the dark he could just about make out two obsidian black deities, fangs bared and daggers in their claws. He had seen them a thousand times before but at that moment it was as if they were now looking at him for the first time. It was then he realised he was not in his monastery, not even in Tibet but over a thousand miles away, in Bhutan, at the Tigers Nest of the noble Guru Rinpoche. He could only reason that he surely must still be meditating? Then, in his doubt, he felt the shade of Guru Rinpoche beside him. The chill, not just on his feet, cascaded over his entire body as he heard Guru Rinpohe clearly whisper:

'Chogyam Trungpa shall have to meditate on what is temporal and on what is eternal.'

Nervous but still bold and a little incredulous, he decided to test the lucidness of what was before him and so he got up and first walked towards and then out the red imperial doors, peered and then looked at the deep forested ascent; he could tangibly breathe in the fresh smell of mountain pine. He then stared at the long pathway to its summit, that swirled in a vertigo beneath him, partially hidden by the dense overhang of vegetation and the span of the high gradient of trees. Then, he saw it. He saw what he thought was a Yeti. It glared at him as a dog began to bark in the valley below. And then he looked down in the direction of the barking, but no dog, and then returned his gaze to his original point, but then no Yeti? But the sound of the dog was getting closer and louder and then it was beside him, directly outside. It broke his meditation, back to his present reality, and present time events; his hand reached out to touch the adjacent temple wall where he had originally sat hours before, not impossibly in Bhutan, but concretely in Tibet. Chogyam, now clearly awake, got up, and ran to his actual temple doors. The dog was barking wildly in the dusk at a Shatom, a bear that would gladly attack humans, a real man-eater, at least Chogyam thought it was a bear, it was standing up, with its front legs, strangely over long, hanging by its side, growling at the now whimpering dog. Chogyam tried to shout for help but his mouth was dry, and as he began stupidly thinking he needed a drink, his friend Akong ran up and started waving a broom at the beast and then shoved Chogyam back inside the temple and slammed the doors closed. Chogyam reached for the small bottle he kept by the burning butter lamps by the garlanded golden buddha. The young monk ignored Chogyam openly swigging alcohol in the temple, he was too busy jumping and shouting 'YETI! YETI!' Then more shouting and commotion was coming from outside, drowning out the excited Akong, hoarser voices of elder monks first screaming and then shouting: 'Run! Run! The PLA is here, the Chinese People's Liberation Army are coming!

Chogyam was drinking alcohol in the holy shrine and not just for courage to break into the Oracle chest or to unfurl the thangka or because he might have witnessed a Yeti. At the age of eleven he could be considered a tearaway, a rebellious kid and he was clearly those things, yet Chogyam was other things too. He was very wise beyond his years. Somehow, he managed to navigate the seemingly contradictory states of wisdom and wilful rebellion. In more advanced years, his disciples said he was practising an ancient tradition which seemed to sum up these oppositional states well: 'Crazy Wisdom'. Indeed Chogyamwas often referred to by his friends and fellow monks as Mr Crazy Wisdom but aged eleven in the temple, the elder monks simply referred to him as 'The Holy Terror'.

Others felt he had led a charmed life but this was itself contradictory, for he had set out on life's path from dire beginnings even before his birth that seemed to deteriorate as he vacated his mother's womb. Born in a cattle shed, his mother lived in a tent made of yak hair with his sister; his real father had left his mother before he was born; his mother married again with Chogyam still in her belly. When he was one year old, monks at a monastery in Surmang in the north-east of Tibet set out on a long journey with sketchy information from a disjointed dream that was teased out in the waking hours of a vision quest. Under such hopeless odds they came looking for the reincarnation of the Supreme Abbot, and found the infant Chokyi Gyatso that would soon become Chogyam Trungpa. Years later even Chogyam would recount how it all seemed rather vague. Regardless, before his mother had given birth his real father had left him and now he had been taken from his mother by a group of strange men. In the monastery away from his sister and mother, in a claustrophobic community of male adults he and his young brethren were at the mercy of all kinds of everything when away from more compassionate eyes. Now just a few years later and whilst still barely out of his youth, his country was being invaded by a mighty foe and he had become a refugee, forced to go into hiding during a harsh winter that turned into another season, then a year, then several more. He finally received news that his monastery had been destroyed by the Chinese People's Liberation

Army. He decided to escape the occupation and leave Tibet. He set off with a ragged group of elderly, women, children, yak herders and his long-time companion and fellow monk, Akong. They came under heavy machine–gun fire crossing a treacherous river, before trekking 19,000 feet across the vast mountains of the Himalaya, sometimes travelling at night, through untracked mountain wilderness. They heard strange noises in the remote mountain passes, but they were scared and desperate and did not trust their ears or their minds. They ate their leather bags and belts in order to survive starvation. When they arrived in India only 13 were left of the 300 who had set out. Chogyam was transported with Akong to a refugee camp run by a wise woman whom he liked, but within three more years they were refugees once more, arriving first in Oxford, England. Akong, with his broken English, managed to get a poorly paid job as a hospital porter and struggled to support both himself and Chogyam with his pittance. Fed up, they both left England when told Britain's Himalayas stood far to the north, and in a roll of the dice and in hope and desperation, headed to the wilds of Scotland, alighting in a run-down hunting lodge amongst wet moorlands and grazing sheep. They convinced themselves that they were both supposed to be teaching the dharma, after all that is what Buddhist monks ought to do, but they were refugees in trauma and barely out of their teens and argued amongst themselves openly in front of the incredulous inhabitants of the tiny Scottish hamlet. It was now the 60s and Britain was beginning to swing; they were supposed to be offering spiritual activities but they only had hippies and the odd rock star. A young David Bowie had found his way there, but he had, for the first time, abandoned his stage name and arrived as David Jones seeking guidance for his identity crises, and carried a book by C. G. Jung on archetypes. The advice he got from Chogyam was unexpected: he told him to embrace his personae like sacred avatars of discontentment.

A young Leonard Cohen also appeared and wisely chose to live at Garvald House away from the excess of the hunting lodge. He left still unhappy and unfixed but he did manage to remember something that Chogyam had said to him entirely out of context; it was not even spiritual advice as far as Cohen was concerned but he used it in a song later. Cohen complained about the broken shutters that would only open a few inches for ventilation at the modest house. Trungpa had replied, 'The cracks, is how the light gets in.'

The general haphazard nature of the retreat would have been enough to drive anyone to drink and one rare balmy Scottish Saturday night, Chogyam did just that—both drunk and possibly slightly stoned—he fell asleep at the wheel of an open top sports car with a girl beside him and crashed into the window of the only joke shop in Dumfries. The sight that greeted the rural backwater police and emergency services at the scene must have been surreal, a Buddhist monk drunk at the wheel inside a broken glass joke shop window. A few days before he had successfully hidden in a stable not too different to the one he was born in when the local police raided the lodge in a hippie drug bust. The locals had had enough, Akong had had enough. Chogyam had had enough, yet at the same time he was clearly medicating his trauma with alcohol and his grief with his Buddhist practice, a kind of karmic sublime, his lived short life seemingly thus far at least a perfect segue of crazy and wisdom. Chogyam was, even at the age of thirty, still recovering from being born.

Then a postcard arrived from two academics in America. It had a faded colour picture of the Rockies and was an invitation to come talk at a seminar, maybe stay a couple of weeks. He became a refugee once more and headed to America, to escape the unwanted press and police attention, but more so, he desperately needed some space from his friend and compatriot

Akong who was now exhausted and had lost his patience. He would look for Shambhala anew, amongst the Himalaya of North America, beginning at the Southern Rocky Mountains of Colorado.

Real Wild Child

The two University of Colorado professors, one a philosopher and the other a mathematician, who had sent a postcard to a Buddhist monk in Scotland featuring a washed-out colour image of the Rocky Mountains, had suggested that he might appreciate the similarity of Colorado to the mountains of Tibet. They heard nothing back and were beginning to give up on the idea, thinking that Chogyam Trungpa Rinpoche was so underwhelmed by the offer he was not even interested enough to respond. However, Trungpa Rinpoche finally replied that he would be coming for a much more extended time than was proposed. Then out of the blue two monks arrived to say Trungpa was coming but it was important that they dispel any preconceived notions of this Rinpoche as a holy being or spiritually pure monk in the way the West had romanticised via Hollywood and films like Lost Horizon. The two professors, part intrigued about the real identity of whom they invited and the honesty of what they had heard, shared what they had been told and began to tell any potential students that Trungpa Rinpoche drank alcohol, smoked cigarettes, engaged in sex, and was really very much like, well, his fellow students. In the autumn of 1970, Chogyam Trungpa Rinpoche arrived in Denver.

He parked himself up in a small cabin located at an altitude of 10,000 feet in the mountains above Boulder, overlooking the snow peaks of the Colorado Rockies. So remote that it had no running water or plumbing, and no electricity or heating, other than a wood stove. The invitation from America could not have come at a more opportune time. He desperately needed to escape Scotland, he had fallen out badly with his old friend and fellow monk and was getting attention from the local police: it was a notoriety had had not bargained for, even given his haphazard life thus far. In addition, he had been severely injured in the car accident only months before, even walking took great effort. He sat in his new home, alone, and just stared out the log cabin window at the mountains, a little sorry for himself and thinking of his fate and feeling a faint ember of optimism, whilst contemplating his new life, the opportunity to begin again. It was true, the Rockies were not unlike the Himalaya, he thought, even more so than the mountains of Scotland. For here he could imagine a stupa, a yak, a wild ass, a bear. He confirmed to himself that they even had eagles, grizzly and black bears, lynx, bobcat, and mountain lions in the Rockies; some claimed they had heard wolves as well.

That was when he saw it, the back of a bear standing on its hind legs, moving out of the aspen and spruce-pines into a small narrow clearing between adjacent pines in the alpine meadow, but, it was moving forward and not by going down on all fours, it was walking upright. It was big, very big. Then he noticed the front legs hanging beside it, but they seemed far longer than the back legs and were more like long, long arms. It looked like, well, it looked like a Yeti. But he surmised there were no Yeti in North America. He looked again and it was still upright, clearly walking but its back remained to him and now disappearing into the trees.

With difficulty, he unrolled the large thangka, the Tibetan religious painted scroll he was given by the Queen Mother of Bhutan, of the Buddha Amitābha, the Buddha of the West. At once he looked for an image of the Yeti in the scroll, but then his mind became diverted and he decided at once, and as he always wished, that he would reclaim the Shambhala teachings, not as he had originally thought in the East but in America, in the West, and that he would call this new place of teaching Shambhala. He was excited and invigorated, and had a drink to celebrate.

Ross and Ruth and I decided that 1980s summer on the long drive; it took two whole days in the end, with a stopover in a motel before we arrived at Shambhala. Along the way Ruth would break into prayer, either reciting by rote or reading from the small Bible she carried in her handbag. It would happen unexpectedly; I found no logic to what would inspire her to do so. I shared the driving with Ross and more than once I found her eyeballing me as she recited a prayer and once she caught me catching her, but I sensed her eyes were waiting for mine as I checked the rear-view mirror when she was reciting the Sermon on the Mount, 'Blessed are the pure in heart, for they shall see God.' I looked back as I was more reminded of Leo Tolstoy's writings than Christ's teachings, but Ruth held me fast long enough that my mind must have wandered into auto-pilot as I was paying no attention to the road: 'You are the light of the world. A city that is set on a hill cannot be hid.'

My gaze was broken by the sound of a large klaxon from an oncoming truck that swerved to miss me, 'Jesus!' Ross screamed, 'What on earth?! Keep your eyes on the road for god's sake. You tired?—Let me drive.'

'It's OK,' I said. 'I saw him,' but the truth was I did not.

Ruth just stared out the window in silence. Then, from the back she said, 'When you look into the abyss, the abyss looks right back.' After ten, maybe fifteen minutes, it began to drizzle, I saw a lay-by and stopped. 'Maybe I am tired,' I offered. Ruth said, 'And the rain descended, and the floods came, and the winds blew, and beat upon that house; and it fell not, for it was founded upon a rock.' 'Jeez Ruth, that's enough. We are not in Bible class,' Ross protested. We all sat in silence.

'Let's rest a while,' I said. Ruth said something unintelligible first under a breath. Then she said, 'There she blows,' and she wound down the rear window and pointed into the woods.

Beside us above and below lay a black wood, on the steep incline of the mountain road. Our small pick-up seemed to reduce in scale as did, here and there, isolated pines that wandered in like stray sheep from the mountains into the pit of the valley and we nestled along the thin line of tarmac road that cut its way through. The pines seemed halted by the black oak, trapped, never to leave. The yellow furze here and there along its border only served to illuminate its dark density. There seemed a vast loneliness in this black wood. And I could just see a dark serpentine river below, that had cut the deep gorge of the valley and that seemed to be accelerating in movement and volume, and each passing second fed by the heavy rain that was falling elsewhere. I wound down my window and the wind was up and it ran the flanks of the first line of trees as they stood sentinel at the breach of the river. Its vertigo rose up to us from the vast fall below. I stared hard at those dark oaks, guarding each and every possible entrance, supporting one another in their resistance, against something, against it seemed us.

In spite of the blustering wind filling the pick-up, the branches did not move, but the leaves shook, and clouds upon piled-up clouds seemed to lay at this very point, arrested in their passage, held up in that dark oak cul-de-sac. There was no heavy rain yet, but the threat was there and it was about to deliver. We all looked and waited. Then my mind was off, like a fool, dashing down into the rocks, falling into the black dark wooded valley, and into the river and wilfully into the black, like Saturn devouring its children. I was ecstatic as beauty was there too, and it called to me. Then the ground shook in a low long rumble, tumbling the resonance of thunder beyond the hills and mountains towards us. The wind slithered now at great speed through the wood and there were bright flashes on the horizon. Day had become night. 'Eve is here,' said Ruth, and then all the water, at once, was unleashed from the mountain gridlock of piled clouds, the road in front of us disappeared in the great torrent and even the trees beside us transferred into a watery blur as if we were nestled inside the arch of a great waterfall. I first thought I heard thunder directly above us, but something large and heavy had fallen behind us; as the rain finally eased I could make out a great tree across the mountain road a few feet from the rear of our car and rocks and a mud slide piled beside it.

We finally arrived and saw the sign for The Rocky Mountain Shambhala Centre and got the time and directions to a seminar that Jo would be at, led by Chogyam Trungpa Rinpoche.

That hot afternoon we walked into a packed hot and smelly room of body odour and waxed wooden floors, with everyone seated or on the floor as the teaching seminar was about to begin. Chogyam Trungpa Rinpoche was small and a little overweight, shoehorned into a shiny slate-grey suit. He was sweating. But despite his unlikely attire for a revered Buddhist monk, he radiated an energy. A kind of high fully turned-on vibrational frequency. I struggled at first to locate it: was it partly with his adoring disciples or was it him? He was as baffling as his appearance was at complete odds with his being. Students asked him questions and he replied. Often disarming their nervousness with a cheeky smile and some gentle humour, teasing himself as much as them. I plucked up the courage to put my hand up to ask a question. He motioned me to stand up and speak. I don't know what possessed me, my own nervousness completely diverted what I wanted to ask him, which was if he was happy now in America as I knew he had lost his home, many he grew up with were imprisoned or were dead and he had not seen those he loved and grew up with in many years, he was still a young man after all. But I forgot all of this, lost my reason and instead as I looked at him, he seemed to be instead looking and smiling at Ruth, and I blurted out, 'Did you ever see a Yeti when you were in Tibet?' Laughter erupted amongst all the students, except Chogyam Trungpa Rinpoche. The laughter stopped and Chogyam Trungpa said, 'No, not in Tibet with my own eyes, or maybe once meditating, but that was in Bhutan, but yes a friend did, and I believe him.'

There was silence. Then Trungpa looked at me again and said, 'But I have seen a Yeti in America.' Everyone started laughing again. I sat down, until the laughter stopped and felt idiotic. But Trunpa continued, 'I saw a Yeti right here,' and he motioned out of the window. More laughter again. But Trungpa said, 'I saw a Yeti in the mountains.' Even more laughter. Then Trungpa who was not laughing as he did before in the questions waited for it to die down. Then he said, 'It's true!' They laughed again. For the first time I saw Trungpa Rinpoche looking very serious and he said, 'I am not joking, I saw a Yeti, in the Rockies when I first arrived,' and he stood and motioned out towards the windows and the direction of the mountains. More laughter. 'I find westerners very confusing sometimes,' Trungpa sighed. And they all laughed even harder.

CHAPTER FIVE

Mistress of the Beasts

'Will you go to Circe's hall? Swine, wolves, and lions she will make us all, beasts of her courtyard bound by her enchantment.'

—Homer, The Odyssey

Inside China, on the border with Tibet, in a valley, amongst a scattering of smaller moon lakes, beneath a sacred mountain resides The Kingdom of Women. The Mosuo tribe—the last such matriarchal, matrilineal society on earth.

The women live independently of their husbands. All rights in any way related to property, money, land and children rest with the formidable Mosuo women. Women choose their own lovers from men within the tribe but are beholden to none.

Ama, the grand matriarch and sorceress, would, on special occasions bring out and wear her bone apron.

She was not someone you would want to ever fall out with. Rumours abound of bad luck, illness and death around those that were unfortunate enough to end up on the wrong side of her. If this was true or not or if she encouraged this was asked of her by her own granddaughter Lazo one day, and even though Lazo was just six she still got a fierce look from her grandmother Ama for daring to ask such a question,

'You should know that's a stupid question the menfolk ask themselves.'

'Why?' persisted Lazo.

'I don't ask questions, no need, as I just know.'

Lazo persisted 'Did you ever curse anyone?'

'All curses are earned, so if I did then they deserved it. Besides I am not the author of anyone's fate.'

Anyone would have wondered way Ama was so specific and vague at the same time with her. But Lazo was used to it, this was how Ama always spoke in response to anything.

'...Well ... did you?' Lazo still tried.

'What do you believe?' said Ama.

Lazo had picked up some tricks from her grandmother so knew sometimes it was a good idea to answer a question with the same question thrown back. 'Do you believe it?' she said.

Ama got animated and started pointing at the mountain.

'We have Gamu the goddess of the sacred mountain to believe in, we have the goddess of the moon lakes, we have the goddess of the mother lakes, we have the spirits of the trees to believe in, we have 400 gods and spirits running around. My grandmother who taught me to be a sorceress and gave me her bone apron, said it was part made from the sky burial bones of her grandmother, after a blue bear that fed on the tiny meat of her shell and the vultures had finished with it. When she went to fetch the bones as her grandmother told her to do so, once it had been picked clean after a year, and make the apron on a full moon ... well, she said she saw a hairy beast walking, first on all fours, but then it stood on two legs, not a blue bear standing, mind, as it had a monkey man face, then it started walking, but not like a monkey, but as a beast walking like us, a Yeti. Anyway with 400 gods and spirits to believe in and the countless demons that outnumber the people, what is one hairy beast of the mountains to add in there? Anyway, who gives a toss about curses, let's believe in it all or not at all!'

'So you don't believe in any of it?' Lazo asked.

'Well, as for curses and ghosts and demons, it's the living one needs to be wary of, not the dead. The bone apron of my great, great grandmother that I wear sometimes, it is useless really. And she told me that when she gave it to me and she was told the same by her grandmother. They both knew that it was just dressing up, useful for scaring the menfolk and the gullible and greedy and keeping them in their place. It was my grandmother—but not my mother, nor your mother—who was a witch. When I was your age I asked my grandmother the same thing, as my daughter, who is your mother was just the same as my mother. There was no point in asking her anything, or you would get: a wild ass is a wild ass, a tree is wood for burning, the lake is cold, the stars in the sky shine for no one, I married the wrong man, the sun is too hot, I am too fat, you are just like your father … etc, etc …' Lazo nodded her resigned agreement.

'Now this is important, and I am only going to say it once, so you better be listening well, and I am only going to whisper it to you, so listen very carefully.'

Ama groaned as she picked Lazo up, complaining a little and for the first time she cursed her failing body. She gently cupped her hand over Lazo's ear, but firmly turned her to face the mountain.

Lazo stared out and was attentive as her grandmother whispered her words. 'In the pines by the lakes, by the Yunnan hills, there is a pine mushroom in the forests, it's prized by foreigners who live on islands amongst the ocean of the world, one day you might see that ocean Lazo …'

Ama paused a while, but Lazo knew she had more to whisper, so she stood silently staring out and finally Ama leant forward once more.

'Do you know what the ocean of the world sounds like? It has a sound no poet can capture, nor musician play, or artist paint and to sculpt it is folly, it is like the greatest of singular mountains that dwarfs all the mountain ranges on earth, and it is a mountain that moves. The sacred mountains and all the mountains of the world have rains and springs and rivers that must all run to it, and run they do above the great mother of the earth or beneath her, the clouds only dance to feed her and the snows and ice only freeze so they may wait on her. The mountains of our world only climbed this high so they could see her, but the ocean slips away falling off the edge of the vision of their summit, the same is true of even

Chomolungma, the great mother and the greatest mountain at the centre of the range of her sisters—so they stopped climbing and they wept the rivers, snow and ice, and all our lakes. I can't see the great ocean Lazo, nor can you, but I know it's there. I don't need to believe it.'

'The hairy beast grandma?'

Ama stopped whispering and turned and stood back to face the mountain with Lazo.

'The snow leopard is out there. I have never seen one, but I found the skull of one and made some medicine from it. I have seen a Tsatom, the plant eater bear, more than once, which is harmless, but not if she has young. Only just once have I seen the man-eater Shatom, after her winter sleep, she was hungry and I knew to keep my distance. I have not seen the Yeti but I saw some tracks in the snow, they were like naked feet and they went on and upwards to a treacherous path and disappeared. They did not disappear from sight, they just ended in the middle of the high snowfield without turning or tracking back; there was a great fissure in the icefall and then beyond I thought I could see some more again.

'But then one day I saw the great bearded vulture by a sky burial in the winter, it was circling and came down in the snowfield, landing in the middle at the north of a pass too hazardous to reach, then it bounded, hopped on its two legs twenty paces before it flew off. By the time I got to the tracks the high sun was burning and the edges of the tracks were melting; they looked odd like the appearing and vanishing track I came across once before. Sometimes even when you look hard and long the truth escapes us.'

'So do you believe, grandma?'

'My grandmother knew it was real, as she wept when she saw it. It's best like the ocean and the snow leopard and the bearded vulture, to know and not to believe and why not? Most people don't care about much, just what's in front of their gaze or what they think they want that they don't really need. Others have too much, but it's never enough, and most forget their ancestors and never give them another thought. Imagine all those that have been on the great journey before us and managed to laugh even though they suffered. At least my grandmother cared enough to wear the bones of her grandmother, not all the time, mind, just when she felt like it or the need arose. But when I put on grandma's bone apron I can get others to believe in curses!'

Ama screamed and clawed at her with her hands and Lazo laughed.

CHAPTER SIX

Mountains as women

The Sherpa that inhabit the lands that run off the base of the Himalaya do not have a word for the top or the summit of a mountain, only for the mountains themselves, the highest of which, the greatest of which, they honour with a feminine name, Holy Mother.

Women inhabit mountains and the great mountain, Mount Everest itself, is referred to as Holy Mother. It did have several other local names before being named Everest after the Welsh surveyor Sir George Everest who strongly objected to any attempt to it being named after him. He sensibly protested that his surname had no equivalent in Hindu and that its correct height was calculated by an Indian mathematician Radhanath Sikdar, who had himself started a journal in 1854 for the education and empowerment of women. Sikdar's credit for writing the complex and technical aspects of the great survey manual was erased by his colonial masters. George Everest extolled and supported Sikdar but it did not get him far, neither did his explicit request that on no account should the Holy Mother be named after him. It was ignored by his successor as Surveyor General of India and by the Royal Geographical Society and so to his total embarrassment it became known as Mount Everest.

The great mountain and those around it in the vast Himalaya are no respecters of gender and claim lives without fear or favour. However, when women die on the mountain they largely remain anonymous. The names of the great mountaineers, the living and the frozen and broken dead, are a long roll of honour, an exclusive call list of men. When alive and kicking and climbing, women remain anonymous—they are our living Yeti beside us, they remain invisible and absent from any concretised record.

In our current world, off the mountains, no one really knows her name, but she is a Nepalese woman who summitted Mount Everest seven times. The most of any woman in the world and many more times than any male mountaineers with western equipment manage. Her little sister, Mingma or Ming Kipa, reached the summit when she was just fifteen years of age. At the time she was the youngest person ever to do so. Her elder sister has three children and her name is Lhakpa Sherpa and she has climbed Everest more than any other woman alive. As a child she often went on dangerous and remote hikes and climbs and got a job as a cook, carrying the loads of other climbers. One day still in her teens she was carrying too heavy a load of tents, food and sleeping bags for an all male Army expedition on thin ice and then she got her foot stuck between two rocks and fell and broke her femur on her upper left thigh. It took her two weeks to get back to Kathmandu where doctors had to cut into her swollen wounds and let them drain. For three days on the mountain she walked wounded. She was given basic medical care, she could not afford painkilling drugs or antibiotics. She was forced to sell her only possessions, her treasured gold earrings, for which she received a mere $10. She received no help or enquiry post her injury from the Army team. The next year she was back on the mountain as a porter but something inside her told her to climb the mountain herself. Having little money she borrowed climbing equipment and set out. Despite all her accomplishments she says that although outside she may appear happy and is smiling, inside she is very sad. The vast mountain is often a mirror to a vast sadness inside.

Another young Nepalese woman, Churim, was the first person to have climbed Mount Everest twice in the same season. She managed this extraordinary feat within one week and dedicated it to another woman, Passang Lhamu Sherpa, who was the very first Nepalese woman to climb Mount Everest; she died on the descent. Again, outside Nepal no one knows her name and little is reported of these inspiring feats.

Is it because the local people on the mountain are perceived as a workforce and a homogenous group of carriers and fixers and cooks and even sometimes for just casual physical comfort? Is it because those temporary visitors from outside know, like the rubbish that remains entombed by their countless expeditions, the locals always remain left behind as well?

Or is it because the Sherpa are so expert at getting to the summit that they dissolve into an anonymous collective? As for the women amongst them—like the Yeti—they are even more invisible, for nobody even bothers to photograph their tracks.

CHAPTER SEVEN

In the beginning was the garden

The first time he saw her, he knew that he was in love.
A song was going through his mind,

'Break on through to the other side.'

And all the while his neighbour's beatbox pumped out. The soundtrack was in perfect symmetrical stereo, *The Doors* in his mind *and* his ears.

He held Eve. He had picked her up at the drugstore.

'Come,' she seemed to say.

'I love you,' she seemed to say.

He called out her name, 'Eve.' But Eve was just a cover girl on the magazine he held.

For $300 a month you get what you pay for—maybe a little less. The Kenmore Hall Hotel—this was his home. One of the few places where somebody, anybody could afford to live, hovering above the poverty line or drowning below on a welfare cheque. Its interior could be summed up in three words: grimy, dirty, ugly. His room housed a bed, mirror and sink. A raw pipe stuck out at the head of the bed with a fire sprinkler on the end. His only concession to comfort being that he had stretched his budget to a room that did not face the main road. However, there was no closet. There was no carpet. Thick heavy brown paint provided the floor covering. A single picture hung above the sink, yet it contained no image, no pastoral scene, just some embroidered words, boxed in a cheap faded plywood frame.

You are not heads to them,
Brains that can think.
You are not hearts to them that can feel.
You are hands.

When he returned each day, he became engulfed by those words—as he scrubbed the dirt from his forearms, from his fingers, from those hands. He just about got by on some casual employment as a gardener at a large estate in Pasadena. The journey to work was long and took the best part of his pay cheque. He, however, would have worked for nothing. He enjoyed planting the soil, disturbing the earth, attending the gardens at Falling Water. In a way they were his gardens, 'Not nobody's, not anybody's, not even the old man's,' he would tell himself. All of this, in his mind, seemed to be confirmed by the fact that in over five years of employment he had never set foot in the main house. He had only seen the old man once, watching from the window of the southern block. That one time he stood and stared at the old man, who looked down and stared back; it seemed to go on for some time, like a child exchanging a long look with another child. Then together, as if it had never happened, they both turned and stared at the mountain range.

That morning the maid had telephoned him at Kenmore. Before he could make the call, the crack-head down the hallway had picked up the pay phone; he cursed her and started bawling that he didn't work for anyone, 'out of principle', and that he was no 'faggot gardener'. When he finally took the call, the crack-head continued to hassle him, 'Some crystal meth?'

Despite his neighbour's aggressive proximity, and between rebuttals, he tried to explain the misunderstanding to Eva and then to vainly tell her that the lizards were indigenous, a protected rare species. She insisted that if he didn't come over immediately she would get the old man to fire him. He stalled her by saying he would ring pest control. He replaced the receiver slowly and gave the crack-head his Collins Correctional Facility stare. The man recognised something, 'Sorry man, what's that fancy word? Is that your *lady*?' He ignored him and as he walked away, as if by apology, the man called out, 'Been homeless most of the time, lot a drinking, lot of pot smoking, you know, the chronic?' As he closed the door on his room, he could still hear him calling out, 'Hey! The meth, it's good.'

That was yesterday. Today, he had to supplement his meagre pay cheque. He exited the Kenmore Hall and hailed a taxi. The yellow cab's lazy approach to the sidewalk gave him enough time to take in its missing front fender and the decapitated plastic Madonna hanging from the front grille.

Inside his ride the faint sound of the Beach Boys piped through the speakers of the driver's cabin. As he listened, an interview with the singer Brian Wilson was going out live amongst a segue of Beach Boys hits: 'Definitely,' said the radio, 'and God comes up a lot in Beach Boy's songs. It has been said that "*God Only Knows*" was the first pop song to have God in the title. What do you think about God?'

'About God?' said Brian Wilson.

'Yeah!' replied the radio.

As he looked through the grubby glass of the passenger window, to his left, on the hill, was a message,

> *Miracle—You make it happen.*

One more dead actress had been posthumously co-opted, and now her monochrome eyes gazed into the distance from a billboard on a slope of pine trees. Above her, on an inconsequential hill, a ludicrous label called out the incantation: *HOLLYWOOD.*

The platinum actress stared. Beyond, lay the citadel—Los Angeles sat squat, almost sterile in the basin, patiently waiting for a stranger to stumble upon it, waiting to tell that stranger: *Miracle—you make it happen.*

He, however, was immune to the advertising. He had ignored the large billboard as he stepped out of the taxi and made his way to the entrance of the run-down hotel. His gaze fell on a pug dog defecating in a hydrangea bush. He watched the entire black stool emerge and flop to the ground. Then the flat faced mutt turned to gaze mindlessly back.

He pushed at the doorway, its glass body obscured by a myriad of credit card logos and the abstract imprint of countless sweated hands. He walked through the empty lobby and over to the elevators. He always imagined he was ascending a great mountain on the roof of the world when he entered an elevator, it was one of the tricks he played to remain sane. He entered an open lift and pressed a faded seven. Once inside the lift, he became just another component: the lever, the wheel and axle, the pulley, the inclined plane, the wedge and screw rope, the fibre rope into metal cable; wheels into various kinds of interactions and ratios between geared wheels; then alloys along the castings and guide rails. Finally pieces engaged. Motion. As it shunted upwards, a stench of stale urine permeated the air. Bending down he stared at a discarded magazine, the glossy pages still inviting, though pasted to the lift floor by an adhesive of root beer and piss; he could make out part of the copy:

> *"... When the winter collections took place nobody wondered whether the designers at Prada, Louis Vuitton, Gucci, Fendi, Yohji Yamamoto, Max Mara..."*

He glanced at the impossibly thin Caucasian girls, porcelain mannequins with soulless eyes; *always the same girls, always the same eyes*. He gazed at the pure clear blues, greens, digitally enhanced whites.

He looked at an ad with a fantasy ski couple holding each other against a pristine backdrop of faux snow-capped mountains, laughing as if their lives depended on it. Their fresh from the-box fashion/utility clothing looked unused and it promised it would remain forever thus. The models were photoshopped, the backdrop stock and part CGI. He became conscious of his own eyes, as they fell on the rising elevator walls and alighted on the gum and graffiti: 'AIDS Cures Fags' in black and another, 'Ranging over the earth, from end to end—Parkside Killas'. Then finally before the elevator doors separated, 'In the beginning was the garden. Then Cain murdered Abel. The first murderer founded the first city' crudely scratched into the alloy above the maximum load-bearing plate.

He walked in and found his appointment rearranging the furniture in the vast apartment, so he could make room to lay out paper press cuttings on the floor. Across the floor were heaps of press reports, disturbed piles of magazine articles, loosely arranged piles of books. He could just make out some articles: 'BIGFOOT was my Lover', from the National Enquirer, 'BIGFOOT witnessed following strange lights', from UFO monthly, 'Is BIGFOOT Vegan?' from a Health and Fitness magazine.

The man looked up, and said as if they may have known each other, 'I want you to hunt and kill Bigfoot. Don't worry it's not murder, it's like a biology vivisection class, we need one hundred percent proof, it's the only way, science needs a body.'

CHAPTER EIGHT

He who sees the unknown

ENKIDU and the Epic of Gilgamesh 2,300 BCE.

Enkidu was powerful and fierce. Hair covered his body, hair grew thick on his head and arms and hung down to his waist, like a woman's. He roamed all over the wilderness, naked, and far from the cities of men. He ate grass with gazelles and grazed as other animals, and when thirsty, he drank from the waterholes, kneeling beside the antelope and deer.

One day, a human hunting and trapping animals saw him, drinking with the animals at a waterhole. At the astonishing sight of the man-beast Enkidu, the hunter's heart pounded, his face went ashen, his legs trembled and he was numb with terror. Praying he had not been seen and terrified of the man-beast's wrath—fear gripped him like death: had he seen a god?

He went to his father, 'Father, I have seen a savage man-beast that is like a beast yet he walks like a man, he drinks with the animals at the waterhole, he has muscles like rock, a back broad like a mountain. He is swift and powerful, I have seen him outrun the swiftest animals. He lives among them and eats grass with the gazelle. He drinks water from the waterholes like them and does not fear even the lion if it drinks beside him. I cannot approach him, I am in fear. He fills the pits I have dug to trap the animals, he tears out the traps I set, he even frees the animals, so I catch nothing. Is this a bad omen? Is this a task that I must slay him or drive him away?

Enkidu found his serpent and his knowledge in a woman but via a man: Gilgamesh.

Enkidu was born of a mother, he had a father and they came from generations, he had sisters, he had brothers. They remained wild.

CHAPTER NINE

The monkey has no astrology

'There shall be signs in the sun, the moon, and the stars'
—Christ.

Luke 21:24–26

The signs read: 'You Are Here'.

So they contemplated cartography. The maps of the land, maps of the oceans, maps of the stars, musical maps, maps of the mind and body, words as maps, the lexicon of maps, the mathematicus of maps, the map of maps, the mother of all fucker maps. I remembered how the Dr. said, 'A map, in order to be a map, must constitute a minimum of two paths.'

That last day in that lost year, I was on a detour. The Dr. was driving the Pontiac—but not looking at the road, nor at a map—but a book from which he was partly reading aloud, whilst also driving the car. He asked questions to which he also gave the answers—neither waiting nor hinting at any response from me. I was doing my best to ignore him.

'Are you able to describe exactly the arrangement of rooms, including the position of doors, in the Samsas' flat in *Metamorphosis*? Do you know for instance that the first half of Proust's *In Search of Lost Time* was no fairy tale but a morning spent on opium in his brothel in Paris?' I momentarily thought about replying, but he was already into his next sentence.

'Can you trace out the map of Dublin in regard to *Ulysses*? Also in respect of Kafka, can you provide an entomological drawing of Gregor? No, NO, it is not a cockroach; it is a domed beetle. Correct interpretation—translation, is everything, or you will get lost. Ah, here is one: who said "An illiterate, underbred book, the book of a self-taught working man, ultimately nauseating"? It was Virginia Woolf on Joyce's very *Ulysses*. Now do you see?' He was waving a dog-eared book at me, Abominable Snowmen: Legend Come to Life, with one hand, and with the other—hand off the wheel—he was gesticulating and then drawing in the air, with his fingers splayed, then closed, then open—a butterfly. I know this because he is now talking about the microscopic comparison of their gentalia—which, *he assures me,* is how the author and entomologist, in this case Nabokov, distinguished the species of this insect. Then he was onto the dog-eared book: 'You know the author of this wrote the classic natural history book, *How to Know the American Mammals,* Ivan T. Sanderson was no slouch, he spoke the truth.' The only thing that seemed true was the vehicle's steering, which although rudderless managed no deviation, despite its hands-free driver.

'Did you know that Galileo never dismissed man from the centre of cosmology—he did not give man a peripheral role when he removed us from the centre—indeed he put us firmly there—but you know what, we are not the only ones at the centre, there is another, that's right and Ivan T. Sanderson knew, this man beast is dead centre, we branch off.'

Oh shut up, was all I could manage—but I had no courage to speak it out loud, it was just rattling around in my mind. He kept talking and I could only silence him by switching off.

After the second or the seventh turn off from the main road, I started to stir out of my stupor, and I became aware of the landscape he was directing the vehicle in. For a moment I felt as if we had gone through passport control and missed something. I tried to get my bearings; I knew that we had passed south of the Santa Monica Mountains, between Hollywood and Silver Lake and that the last landmark that he had referred to was the Griffith Observatory. I vaguely remember the Dr.'s voice telling me that it was once used to train pilots in the Second World War, and then astronauts from the Apollo programme in celestial navigation. Now I stared at my reflection, fractured in the glass by a decorative bridge, and I instinctively moved back as it seemed to loom out towards the pavement. My mind was elsewhere and nowhere, I followed myself—a face reflected, until it vanished—and then appeared again. *Vanished*—I was losing myself in a moving mirror of reflection: it helped silence him from my head, my deaf phantom was the sole recipient of his endless voice. I felt I was floating free from my body as if the vehicle had crashed and I was hanging onto life. I could hear a siren, police or emergency services floating in the air, up from an adjacent valley. My image became fixed once more in the fabric of a pavilion in the Oriental style as the car cruised and slowed. I concentrated on its turrets, as he eased off the pedal; a faded sign for the A-Z Hotel popped oddly out. By now, he had directed us past home upon home of genteel exclusivity, deep into moneyed real estate.

The mixture of buildings was exotic and the information offered by the Dr. did not stop. He explained that although Beverly Hills was thought by many to be the symbol of luxury living, here in Ranchos Los Feliz lay one of the most exclusive areas of Los Angeles.

'Do you know that buried in these hills, canyons, mountains and valleys, apart from the homes of the elite, are the bones of other beings. The rich even have their very own ark, the Los Angeles zoo. The thing is, in the city that has everything, the dream factory is missing something as they don't have a Squatch. Do you know what a Sasquatch is? Sure as hell they don't. You sure as goddamn know what is one now.'

He drove along Los Feliz Boulevard and finally slowly turned into the driveway of a sumptuous building off Gross Crescent.

The building that greeted us was almost buried like some forgotten Mayan temple and lay amongst two mature grapevines and an impressive willow. It was composed of countless interlocking cubic blocks, each textured and embellished with a highly stylised relief—all individually reminiscent of some deep impenetrable Mesoamerican relief. It looked familiar.

I began to half-recognise the construction, and then it was unmistakable as the light illuminated and the building penetrated the space before us.

Frank Lloyd Wright the Dr. seemed to announce inside my head, then I saw his words leak weakly to his lips in the rear view, and then he declared, 'The Twelfth House.'

And then almost at once, another voice: 'Nature makes me nervous,' She said, opening the door and continued, 'Christ those lizards spook me. The gardener told me they have no eggs, they are actually born live.'

'Excuse me?' the Dr. spoke first.

A petite maid, Mexican, maybe Colombian? I was thinking. She looked familiar and acted like she knew me. The maid ignored his question and continued.

'The gardener gave me your number. Pest control?'

'No? Oh? I should have recognised him, and?'

But I stared blankly and the Dr. ignored her. Then as she ushered us in and closed the door, I could not help but notice the gothic script carved on the inside of the lintel:

California, Sun in Aquarius. Scorpio Rising.

'This way, this way, sorry for the confusion.' She hurried about, her eyes constantly moving and alighting on everything it seemed except us. I, however, could not help but stare boldly at her remarkable face, Colombian I had decided. The Dr. later swore, her lips did not move, only her nostrils, when she spoke. He was right I think.

'It's like a goddamn aquarium. No? I mean, not a zoo, what do you call it? A goddamn snake house. That's what it is.'

'I think you mean a vivarium,' I said.

'Yeah, maybe?' It was now her turn to ignore me and she stared at me blankly. She then gestured upwards and continued, 'He's upstairs. He is not taking the medication you know. I keep finding pills around the house, he's still a nut about the thing he claims he saw. He's got worse since that earthquake on Martin Luther King day.

'Lift every voice and sing, till earth and Heaven ring—he has been to the top of the mountain and now he has shaken it too.'

'What?' I mumbled.

'Northridge earthquake shifted the tectonic plates on MLK Day. Sun is in Capricorn, moon in Pisces, Taurus Rising. With the sun close to the 9th house of higher wisdom, just like the old man, Luther King Junior, was a man who could tune into his vision. Mercury in the 10th house gifts him oratorical powers. Saturn, representing sadness and the end of things is in the house of death. That was his fate, all challenged by oppositional planets ruling firearms and explosions in the 12th house of misfortune. This signals his tragic end at the height of his influence.'

This was one of several visits to a building created by the architect Frank Lloyd Wright that the Dr. had insisted on bringing me to. A month before we had travelled to the Appalachian Mountains and the Bear Run River, the location of Falling Water.

Falling Water was a home like no other.

The architect had built on an ancient native burial ground and wrapped the house around a river. Both within and without it hailed the geomancy of its creator. Wright had caught the falling expanse, negotiating it through a section of the cantilevered balconies and terraces and out through the first floor of limestone and concrete to flow onto the rock escarpment, and then back into the river. The Dr. had told me it was falling in a forever-liquid moment, an always-on rain dance, viviparous and vivid. He then carried on to such an extent—in an endless cliché of all things flowing, saturating, and penetrating that I had to threaten to piss on his shoes in order to make him stop.

But he told me to focus on that, like a meditation, it was far better than medication.

The Dr. insisted that Wright built here and built this house like no other because he had seen something strange on the river. He had seen the beast. The Dr. said it was after the fire and seven violent deaths of Wright's family, staff and workers at Shining Brow or Talisen at Spring Green, Wisconsin one August afternoon. Wright thought he was hallucinating at first; deeply depressed, he was in a state of anxiety, he had had a mental breakdown that was never really dealt with, it just resonated on in waves of grief and regret. The sighting he had might have remained there, just more strange furniture in his head. But Wright had confessed to one of the Native American workers what he saw and he told Wright that what he saw was no illusion. The beast had come to heal him, to make Falling Water on the tribal land; it meant he was given permission, is what he told him. It was a good sign, he told Wright to relax. The house was not a house, it was not a home, it was a gateway. Learn from nature it was telling him. Before it was the Bear Run River it was the Oh Mah or Sasquatch Run River.

'Native American art, all the tribes, the nature of time, its form as they perceived it, not as a human construct but a cosmological one meant they were uncomfortable with the linear nature of time; in their inscriptions, and in other elements of this building that echo their original monuments, they are elucidating the symmetry of time—the cyclical nature and repetition of both time and event. The actions of the tribes were the same as their nature spirit guides, generation after generation to the dawn of their creation myth. This consciousness of the past re-enacted in the present, is everywhere in their art. The tribes watched the heavens with such committed concentration so as to detect the repetitive patterns against which their history took place. Red Elk told me that time pinpoints the sequence in which events unfold and memory takes form. You will meet Red Elk one day.'

He was pleased with this last pronouncement and he stopped talking and seemed to be reflecting on this as if I or indeed someone else had spoken the words.

He took my hand and placed it deep into the surface of the hollow textured brick columns.

'Can you *feel* it? I know you can. Wright developed this building and others with the same complex astrological calendric system in order to locate the events of lives precisely within this temporal framework. It's a gateway. That's why he said architecture was frozen music. He looked at the land and listened to the tribes.'

As I touched the column I wanted it to transmit something back. I wanted to wonder in the same way the Dr. did. I needed to feel something in the fabric of this contemporary construction that echoed the past, really *feel* something—not just simply note the elegant architectural references of its creator Wright. I strained in a hope to sense something—but all was cold, inanimate, useless dull cement. My lack of response did not stop the Dr.

'The essence of native tribal art, inscriptions, totems, masks and architecture was to memorialise the living nature and ensure their place in history within that. Their actions were just re-enactments of cosmic events that occurred deep in the past and by projecting dates forward to our time and beyond, they knew they would be known for millennia.'

I cease hearing and find my gaze wandering through one of the open walls. The wind is blowing and the first leaves of autumn are falling. I want desperately to find some mental space away—but the Dr. keeps on speaking, talking, lecturing, pontificating, questioning. The brief respite is not silence but me tuning into another frequency. The truth is I am not, but everything the Dr. says makes a kind of sense.

I stood looking for more falling leaves and trying not to succumb to the Dr.

'I spoke with Red Elk a year before he died. He said some marks started to appear on stones, strange marks they did not entirely know what they meant. Red Elk thought they were warnings about future times to his people. Some of the tribes said that Oh Mah, the Man of the Mountains had been seen again, but had revealed himself to some of the children, that Sasquatch had been leaving tracks where they could be found, tracks leading to the stones. Red Elk heard of this Buddhist monk in the Rockies and that he should go meet him and show him the markings in the stones. Sometimes all you have is traces to go on. Some of the best of them have left so much written, so many words, and yet they did not write themselves, it's just traces again, *terma* from Guru Rinpoche and Yeshe Tsogyal. We only know of Socrates through Aristotle and Plato. Christ did not write any books. It's strange that everyone around him felt compelled to put pen to paper but Christ in his brief career does not even carve his name in graffiti in a carpentry shop. Literary sources for the life of Mohammed only begin five generations after his death, the Saracen as prophet who comes with sword and chariot as well as peacemaker. Arabia is vast and no real archaeology has taken place there, but it has many mysteries hidden like Petra in the sand to be revealed and dismay us.

'One can't depend on his written words as one would, with say, Dante or Pascal or Aquinas. However, one can say with relative certainty that he was a Jew, that he was a spiritual teacher and that he was put to death by crucifixion. We only have the four gospels. Then we have Paul of course who never met him. Red Elk knew about these teachers of the white man, and he knew they were true as they followed tribal oral tradition: never write anything down, it's only going to get twisted or read in the wrong way. The preachers who read from books had it all wrong, the disciples who wrote the books had it all wrong. You have to show and tell, Red Elk said this all the time. He said the cosmology was how his people were first taught by the Star People. He knew perfectly well what I was talking about when it came to astrology, how useful a true birth date would be. I could ascertain far more about Christ with that one trace, from such a crumb, as to make all the rest ever written about him largely irrelevant. A resurrection date could be of use too.'

But we do know, I told the Dr. That's why we have Christmas Day and Easter? 'Yeah kind of.' It's all there anyway—the Bible—it really is full of astrology. The Magi and the Star of Bethlehem. The old Jewish Temple in Jerusalem with the twelve signs of the Zodiac inlaid into its floor. Saturn is the planet that rules the Hebrews. God is a Capricorn, Christ is Pisces, Satan is Sagittarius, the Demons as fallen angels are Aries, Gemini, Leo, Scorpio. The Angels are Taurus, Cancer, Virgo and Libra, the Antichrist is Aquarius.

Eva the maid appeared again and beckoned us upstairs to see the old man who occupied the building.

As we entered, the old man could hear our voices approaching, but to him it was strange as he thought he recognised one as his own. But he shut them all out. He needed to concentrate: a song was playing as the medication hit in and the morphine ascended to vanquish the pain of his cancer. Not a song inside his head but from the radio of the male nurse along the hallway.

The rhythm helped. The sub-bass frequency submerged through the wooden flooring and found a hollow in his stomach. As the source of the sound passed and its core faded, a separate harmony called from the maid—a sing-song saccharine sound—now high in treble entered his head: 'Sir, the Dr., Sir, the Dr., Sir, is here and …'

The old man wanted to sing along. All his senses were heightened. The smell of his stale urine was enriched and reanimated by at first an internal sensation that was at once externalised as his hot piss flowed effortlessly through the folds of his bed linen. It was not an unpleasant feeling. This incontinence was the failure of innocence, of that of a babe. Yet inside the old man, the temple was corrupted. Within his body was the blood; within this blood was venous claret of USA pharmaceutical inc.: *Toradol* for pain, *Librium* to control his mood swings, *Atvian* for agitation, *Depakote* to counter his acute mania, *Thorazine* for anxiety, *Visaril* for anxiety and *Lorazepam* for anxiety, *Diazepam* and *Valium*. Not just pills, a hypodermic lay deep inside his only withered arm. He was trying not to focus on the medicated soup, he was trying to remember the gateway and think about Falling Water.

Once upstairs, the Dr. dismissed the male nurse and opened and closed the door to the old man's bedroom so quickly that I felt I had negotiated between the hallway and bedroom without taking a single step. Inside, from the floor to the ceiling—a huge decorative map of America lay flush wall to wall, with tiny figures of a hairy bipedal figure—all indicators of a sighting of the man beast, Sasquatch or Bigfoot.

The map, the incapacitated old man, the house, it all felt preternatural. The more I attempted to take it in, the more it seemed to elude me. I could not settle my gaze and just as I seemed at the point of settling down into something, the Dr. interrupted. He had begun to tell me that this body was a city on the edge, an island about to go under, and that although this man was born in *Virgo,* he was now being crushed under the foot of Hercules, in the fourth house of *Cancer.* I then watched as the Dr. began to remove the intravenous drip from the old man's only buckled arm. The skin lay slack along its fragile bone, as if it was no longer held together; and as it fell to the side, it mirrored the disconnected limp tubing of the liquid medication. The Dr. told him to relax in that way that he had—the old man was dead now, or as the Dr. reassured him, 'He would be, any moment now.'

I know I looked agitated. He told me to calm down, and then he proceeded to say in a matter of fact way that the old man was not religious, and therefore would need no rights or prayers to be read. Yet out of respect, the Dr. would tell one final story.

'Alaska and Hawaii are all of course under the piscine zodiac sign. Colorado too is of the 12th sign, Pisces, and this despite the fact it is landlocked. What do you make of that? New York was born under Virgo. Why do you think you have a grid system in New York? Manhattan with block skyscrapers? It is because, any serpentine routes, any deviation in the straight or horizontal or vertical, causes acute anxiety. Typical Virgo, Manhattan loves order. Even though it's chaotic on the surface with human activity, it gives the illusion its conquered nature with order.'

Always remember, you were born, not under, but above the new moon. *I think I heard the Dr. say that, but now I know it was me, I was the old man.*

I felt dizzy. I leant back hoping that a wall was close and would offer some support or that my mother would somehow appear and cradle my fall. Why I was thinking of my mother, I don't know? But there was nothing and as the ceiling came down and the floor up to meet me in a full blown colour kaleidoscope of America, I wished that I had listened more carefully, with full attention to everything the Dr. had been telling me. But most of all I wished that he had never taken that second, or seventh, or tenth turn off from the highway. But was it the turn off? Or was it the car swerving, with me at the wheel, crashing into the steel barrier as my meds kicked in and made me hazy from my cancer treatment, or was it because I was desperately avoiding the large elk that had run out in front of me; itself being chased in fear of its life by a large hairy beast man? A bipedal hairy giant from the edge of the trees caused me to crash and end up bedridden with just my maps and the Dr. and my obsessions? I was back to the logic and order of death, one way, no return, exit. But the Dr. was talking still, I think, and I was back to thinking of New York and my mother, and even though my life changed drastically following the car crash in Northern California.

I was born on the East Coast, in a big city, not under the new moon, but above it, the New Moon Chinese Restaurant in New York. I opened the fortune cookie, it read:

> *'The Monkey has No Astrology.'*

The *New Moon* was, or rather *is*, a Chinese restaurant, located in New York City's Little Italy, for Little Italy and Chinatown blend as does so much in New York. It was a miracle the sign was still there, faded, but still visible beneath the smaller elegant hand-painted sign in fluid Arabic script, that helpfully translated into English the promise of halal meat along with praise to the Prophet.

I did not know why I had come back; it was not as if this exact location could have offered any residual memories. Although I was born here—or so my mother told me—I had no memory of it as an actual home. Yet something drew me here. Maybe it was the streets of the neighbourhood. They did indeed offer a wealth of memories, both good and bad, but mostly bad. New York's little Italy: Mulberry Street, Broome and Canal, all of lower Manhattan, south and west to Lafayette, east to the Bowery and north to Bleecker. Despite the large map in my room attended by nurses and carers, the Dr. would say that I could not read maps, but then no one could.

He would go on to say and that all I—or *you*—might ever hope to know about our journey was the general direction in which we were going. The basic four cardinal points: north, south, east and west was all we could hope to know, and that simply was because of two stars, the North or Pole Star at night and our own rising and setting star at dusk and dawn. Maybe he was right and maybe I knew deep down that was more than enough. The Dr. would tell me the four points of the compass were like the circle of the compass itself and represented totality itself. He knew and Red Elk knew this from their nature and spirit signs and others too: 'These four points are just as in the four sons of Horus, the four seraphim in the vision of Ezekiel, and the four dogs of the Babylonian Marduk or the four symbols of the evangelists or the Four Kings of Buddhism.'

The Dr. said Red Elk told him about the mystery of the moon—that it was no sterile satellite conquered and abandoned by NASA but that it was a cosmological device that controlled the fertility of humankind and animals. In ancient Babylon, he would say, the moon was male. He also assured me most seriously that the moon as well as the sun controlled our weather, it was just we never bothered to investigate the moon in such regard.

The Dr. told me that the grid system, laid out in New York by the city's planners, lulled me and all my fellow New Yorkers into a sense of order, of a false sense of where we were and where we may be going. It was as if the city planners knew that this first city of America needed things under control, for New York would need to plot the way forward for the rest of urban America. New York City would be the New World's way station for the old world—towards its unceasing unsentimental conquest of nature.

I knew he was right, that some semblance of order over nature is all that we could ever hope for. I sensed that we were all just some component part of the microbial anarchy, even in our clean sterile maps of the city. The Dr. said its hard fabric as well as its soft content was as filthy as the dark disturbed earth and its dark pagan forces. *Nature makes us nervous,* he would say. The city too made me deeply uneasy. My maps were a portal of discovery and therefore a form of control, of meaning. 'Columbus did not discover America,' Red Elk told the Dr. 'It was already here.' Even the concept we know as America today could not yet exist in Columbus's mind. I desperately needed something and my maps seemed to hold back the overwhelming modernity and human chaos of it all, by mapping it out in order. The fractured city and its noise, its smells, its visual overload, its inability to switch off: was as wild as the deepest jungle. The maps contained that, kept it at bay. The Dr. would say, why did travellers seek novelty elsewhere, when an undiscovered realm was all around? For in this city on any given day, in any given month, one could witness the world in its entirety and its infinite variety. It would not take long, he would say—it could indeed happen in just one moment.

If one would take the time to stand quiet and motionless, and maybe hold one's breath, on the corner of any street in lower Manhattan, one could witness the world's tidal wave of humanity wash by, and one might hope, in that fleeting breath, to stop it.

And as a child that is exactly what I would do. Stand still, holding my breath and counting, asphyxiating against the human tide—the 11 billion and counting.

As I stood there in late September I was thinking hard, trying to source a memory of the New Moon and my mother beside me, with me above it. Apart from my mother's promise all I have is a very loose, tangential memory of it all. I recall there had been talk of the neighbourhood shrinking and my trying to grasp this. For I knew the city was not shrinking, it was growing; New York City, my city, and all my new maps could not keep up—could not contain it. Indeed I now ventured north to Houston and happened upon new exotica: Chinatown, but I would hear the adults say conversely that it was Chinatown that was coming into us, into Little Italy, as if somehow Little Italy's name held its own stunted stature and forthcoming demise. The new immigrants and their very different ways from the furthest East had arrived and more were coming. They were advancing into the west, the north and south of the city and they were stopping and not moving on. The Dr. said that Red Elk had told him that new people were a portent of change and that change was conversely not them—but us.

I was too young to make any sense of it all but I remember clearly that I grasped something one late cold spring morning. An unknown Chinese man had watched me secretly holding my breath and counting out seconds with nods of my head on the corner of Columbus Park. This stranger surprised me, he came to me and stopped my breathless counting with a sudden firm grip of my arm that arrested the blood and said in excellent English: 'Are you holding your breath for the ghost shadows and counting the dragons?' I answered with a sheepish no. No I was not counting the dragons or ghost shadows, I did not know what those were.

I never saw him again and I never held my breath or counted to stop the city again. Instead I collected the city in maps, anywhere I could find them, gas stations, museums, thrift stores. And when that was not enough I made new maps, my own maps—not the stupid maps that tell you nothing but the old names of streets—but maps that would say that Giuseppe the street vendor was gone from his pitch in the recess of an abandoned building that was empty and that the former Post Office was now a bank or that the Subway was not just the steps down to 33rd Street but also housed the news-stand run by Mr. Shariff from Pakistan, and that the homeless lay there—an alcoholic man called Si and a bag lady who did not know her name or would not own up to it. It was, I suspect, in a kind of Asperger's syndrome of mapping—an attempt to house any detail, no matter how trivial. I tried to forget about the shadows of ghosts or flying dragons or other emotional forces—because I suspected in that lay make-believe and madness. I knew what I recorded was real—but I would later find out—the Dr. said that later, probably too late, I would realise that my lists and my maps in all their details and hard cold facts, were stranger than anything one could ever hallucinate psychotically or imagine cognitively; when looked at anew they would mean nothing, were absurd. The native tribes needed no maps: everything was held in nature, and even the best animal trackers knew all was not as it appeared even in traces, and that the footfall prints of Sasquatch or Bigfoot told them that, that nature held back secrets, so beware. It follows like death, beware.

I recall this as I remember staring at the plastic wallet containing the menu taped on the inside of the smoked glass front of the New Moon. It is still a Chinese Restaurant—despite the Arabic script denoting its observance to Islamic dietary laws. However, there are no pork dishes listed and the meat is halal. The restaurant's patron is a Mr. Hui and it is now named the Zheng

He. Like everything else in China, the scale that we apply in the West is truly off the map. All we have is our numbers—we are told that it is a land of billions and that it is the fastest growing industrial force in the world. The Islamic Chinese are a minority, yet still manage to number some 200 million. Their prophet and intermediary to Allah was a eunuch, and despite his lack of genitals and despite the revolution and the purges, it remained the most resilient of all the faiths in China, and now these very same Islamic Chinese are parked in America in Manhattan's Little Italy, in a pork-free Chinese restaurant, one that serves no rice wine or duck and so it is—it is this now and it was also the building that was my entry into the universe. But I learnt long ago that nothing in New York or for that matter anywhere else was ever as it seemed.

I have also learnt that coincidence is just like reading maps: it arises as simple roads branch into others that then in turn lead back. I no longer comment on coincidence, as its occurrence is as commonplace as to make its definition redundant. But I mentally note that Zheng He was a great Islamic Chinese explorer and map maker too, and that today is the Feast of Saint Gennaro, as it was on the day that I had my accident and saw Bigfoot.

The year 305AD seems a long long time ago to anyone and even more so to someone born in the New World. When someone dies that is it. They are dead. If they died in 305AD like Saint Gennaro, well, they are as dead as anyone can ever imagine—bones turned to dust a millennium ago. But I am on Mulberry Street and it is not 305AD but a long time after and the street is closed to traffic, as a fair is now part of the neighbourhood. It is the Feast of Saint Gennaro and there are parades, street vendors, some with T-shirts one of which says 'Holy Virgin Pray For Us', there are sausages, pizza and zeppole candles and small grottos along the way—here and there and in the most unlikely places, and women in black. Women with the air of the old world about them, talking and praying in thick Neapolitan accents or the parochial accents of the small villages that surround the hills and valleys of the ancient city that sits on the edge of the dormant mountain, the sleeping volcano. And like the magma deep in the earth in that old world, here today is a phial of some dry ancient blood that is about to undergo an annual liquefaction. St Gennaro the patron saint of Naples, Bishop of Benevento, saint and beheaded martyr is here in the form of a polychrome statue, like a vaudeville painted lady, made-up with clown rouge and lipstick. I witness the image of the saint being carried out along the block.

I am well away from the New Moon now and inside Little Italy's version of the grand cathedral of Naples and an archbishop is holding up a glass phial amid the prayers and invocations and is declaring that the dried blood of the ancient saint has liquefied. Back in Naples this announcement would be greeted with a twenty-one gun salute in the 13th century Castel Nouvo—here in Manhattan it is car horns and whoops and I hear a man next to me say in loud impassioned prayer: 'With the assurance of being heard—we implore you to obtain God's mercy for us. Protect your city Naples from the scourge of disbelief.

Amen.'

The church has emptied and so I walk out and purchase a copy of National Geographic and American Gun Magazine, as both promise free fold-out maps on their covers. I open up and read an ad:

> 'People who drive silver or blue cars should not read this. People who are born under the sign of Scorpio or Sagittarius should not read this.'

The map is not the territory. Now there is something else. There is a smell about the city, almost of past ages, the stuff that arises from decay. It's a new city I tell myself, it's New Amsterdam, it's New York, it's Manhattan.'

> *'The hidden history of man can be read*
> from his own structure, which appears
> *as a compendium of the animal realm.'*

'I am *Lenape*. My ancestors sold Manhattan for $24 to your ancestors—but that was way back. Probably get my dreaming from my ancestor Neolin the Delaware Prophet. He was against alcohol, polygamy, materialism and all things European. He wanted a return to the old traditional ways, away from dependency on the settlers.' Neolin the Delaware prophet told me to tell you under the Old Moon it's too late for you to forget your useless white man's map and desire for dominion. Too late to avoid the car crash in your crazy metal horse. You should listen to Pontiac the Ottawa leader not drive one. The hairy man of the mountains always comes at the end times.'

CHAPTER TEN

When the stars …

'Tyger Tyger, burning bright,
In the forests of the night … '

—William Blake

One day Xan awoke and changed his mind about everything.

He had dreamt a strange dream just before dawn, that he was beneath the Tiger's Nest, it was on fire. He saw a man and a woman coming from the flames, riding upon a pregnant tigress and waving a snake as a whip. 'Wángguó!' they both cried.

Wángguó is a Chinese word that expresses loss of country, the threat of extinction.

The young Xan collected things, mostly to do with words, books, poems, newspaper cuttings. When he got his first mobile phone he would sent texts, but they would be so long that his friends said they were far too long to read, so would scroll to the end and ignore the greater part. He was frustrated whenever he got a one-line reply by email or even worse just three words or two or one by text. His friends loved computer gaming and it was the only subject they were happy to talk about at any length by text or email. One morning he changed his mind about everything. He started first by experimenting and sending shorter messages of extracts of poems to his friends. His girlfriend laughed at him once and said instead of writing such long emails and texts, and forget about writing books as books are too long to read, he would be better off writing, you know, fridge magnet poetry, posting pictures on Instagram, get some followers Xan, or it's just not worth it. He told her that trying to express the truth was nuanced and took more complex dialogue. She was not impressed: she told him to '… just make stuff up, pretend you are doing stuff when you are not; most people take one carefully put together photo and use it to build a narrative that they are having a great time, but they are not. You are always complaining Xan, so you are not having a great time anyway, so what's your problem?'

Xan found most women, including his girlfriend, were merciless in getting to the point. He had met Yi playing online. She was very good at gaming. He also liked to mercilessly get to the point but he could only do this by hacking things and in real life he was an outsider, awkward and unsure about everything.

Yi had told Xan that she lived her life entirely online. In the past four years Xan realised that he had never really met Yi. If he did, he pictured her at her laptop or staring at her mobile phone like an open wound in her hand. He imagined her speaking to him sideways so as not to avoid the vanity mirror of her electronic tablet. He would struggle to think of Yi looking up at him, directly. Yi was nothing special in this regard, she was just like almost everyone he knew, except his grandmother and other old people he guessed, but he never met any other old people apart from her. His grandmother was the only person he knew who had a landline. It was useless calling it from his mobile as she was almost deaf and could not hear it ring or he found himself shouting things to her down it: so the conversation always ended up short and confused. When she died he was sure that she would be the last person he knew with a landline and no computer. Xan never bothered to explain the concepts of emails or the internet to his grandmother as he thought it would be useless. But the day before he had his dream he did. His grandmother despite having little clue to technology did have a television but she only watched two things over and over: this was possible as it was really only a monitor for her comfort films that played via a DVD player he bought her one year. But she did read books like Xan and had a very good library in her apartment. She was a romantic communist and despite all the hardships she felt a lot was better in the past. Mao was good for women, she would say, trust me before it was terrible. She also said he was good for nature; she preferred it then as everyone cycled and you could still hear bird song and watch bees gather honey amongst the flowers, even in the big cities. One of the best things about communism was there were few cars she would say. Although she drove a tank. Or she did when she was in the army. It was the only photograph she kept of any kind of a motorised vehicle. She thought about throwing it away after the June 4th Incident—the protests on Tiananmen Square; she had long been out of the army by then—but she said once the young people protested, that was fine, but then they should have gone home; no one respected their elders anymore she complained. She drove a Type 59 tank. Her faded photograph contained a great mass of tanks and armoured vehicles on Tiananmen Square. Below it she had a quote from Mao:

> China is usually subjected to the domination of three systems of authority, political authority, family authority and religious authority. As for women, in addition to being dominated by these three systems of authority, they are also dominated by the men—the authority of the husband. These four authorities—political, family, religious and masculine—are the embodiment of the whole feudal-patriarchal ideology and system.

As there were so many tanks on parade he had to ask her to remind him which one was she driving: it was the far outside one in the third row, but it was more like a ghost he thought, a spectre in the old black and white photograph, consumed in the dust of the preceding columns.

He knew why she loved to watch one particular film, as she was a hopeless romantic—even when it came to Mao and communism. It was a badly dubbed American film, 'The World of Suzie Wong'. She would make him watch it with her when he was very young. It was like a soap opera, but she would always say, even now, if it was on in the background: 'Look at how beautiful Nancy Kwan is, Xan.' The film was excruciatingly embarrassing when he was young, especially as Nancy Kwan played a prostitute to an American imperialist. This explicit contradiction did not seem to bother his grandmother at all. He would blush beside her and she would scream in delight every time William Holden tore off Nancy Kwan's western style dress and exclaimed, 'Wear your own kind of clothing. Oh dear don't try to copy some European girl!' She would drool over 1960s Hong Kong, even though she had never visited it and say, look how beautiful it was, and then complain how terrible it is now, all those new ugly modern buildings and too many cars! This despite the fact she has never been to Hong Kong before or after the British left. She is baffling, but she is mostly right, thought Xan. The other film she adored he loved too. She first came across it in Tibet when she was serving in the army. Avoiding the censor-approved films and always independent, she was so confident in her devotion to Mao she felt no intimidation stepping out of the state-approved loop and found a local film club and saw a screening that entirely recreated the Himalaya, a 1940s film shot entirely in Britain. Again this did not bother her, she said it captured something perfectly about the mountains that no other actual location-shot film could, and only someone who spent time in the real place as she did then would know. She explained to Xan that it worked because the painted backdrops and paper-thin sets, its emptiness, came much closer to the truth that one will never understand the illusion of the mountains. This was the film's blessing she would tell him. Xan was equally enraptured by Black Narcissus, the fact it was directed by two people at the same time, and that they themselves had never been to the Himalaya nor indeed had any of the mostly British cast. The film transported him in a way that made him want to go to the far Himalaya as his grandmother had, but any time he asked his grandmother about Tibet she always had the same stock answer, 'Let's watch Black Narcissus together,' she would say. Yet after, always, they would never talk about the film or indeed Tibet, and yet somehow they were both satisfied with this, as if anything they might say, any critique, would just banish its magic. Until yesterday. Yesterday, after they had watched the film together in silence, Xan made green tea as usual, but then his grandmother suddenly told him to get the Tibetan Book of the Dead down from her bookshelf. It was a Chinese translation containing a psychological commentary by a Swiss psychoanalyst, C.G. Jung. As she held it she said to Xan that the book was a guide to the dead and the dying and that she was maybe closer to this than him, and winked and said,

'But you never know?' She told him she agreed with its commentary as Jung suggested, that it is also a guide to the living. She then told Xan a little of Jung and that she had studied him at length over the years, especially after she discovered his book in an English-run Indian library near the capital in Lhasa and then she captivated Xan with her description of archetypes. How that even Mao was an archetype, Xan was transfixed. She never saw Mao in person to her great and profound regret, she would add, even when she was driving her Type 59 tank. In the pride of place photo she was not one of those saluting eyes right in the turret above, for she had to dutifully keep her line and stare directly ahead, keeping the formal ballet of choreographed power perfectly in line. Then she said that only just once in Tibet, she once saw a miracle, a living archetype high on a mountain pass, near a monastery, the Tigers Nest. 'Was it a holy man?' Xan asked. 'No,' she said and leaned forward and whispered, 'It was like a god, Xan. It was a Yeti.'

They both sat in a long silence following her whispered words. She held the Tibetan Book of the Dead firmly between her hands as if in prayer and told him the book's real title was not as translated but, *The Great Liberation by Hearing in the Intermediate States.*

She knew this because she had been communicated to telepathically by ancient Tibetan adepts immediately that she saw this hairy godlike man, this living archetype like no other, this Yeti high on the mountain. Xan was spellbound, but all of it was just a bit too much and he raised his eyebrows. Seeing this she admitted that she was also unwell from altitude sickness, but that this was also an intermediate state and she hoped he was truly listening.

She said that there was an archetype for everything and that the Yeti was its very own, a most special one. Incredulous, he asked her could there really be an archetype for everything? She firmly answered, 'Yes.'

So to trick her he asked what was the archetype of the internet. She said straight away that she did not know yet and indeed no one knew, but that he, Xan, would find out. 'How?' he asked. It would come to him in an intermediate state, like a dream for instance, she said.

Xan left his grandmother with his head reeling, full of the erotic fantasies of sexually frustrated nuns from Black Narcissus, archetypes, Type 59 tanks, a 1960s Nancy Kwan and all interrupted by a Yeti stomping around in a technicolour landscape.

That night he had the dream that he was by the blazing Tigers Nest. The flames were so intense he could feel the heat on his face. He saw a man and a woman coming from the flames, riding upon a pregnant tigress and waving a snake as a whip, Wángguó! they both cried. Then he saw his grandmother, she was holding a candle and she whispered a poem to him: 'Do not measure the space between stars, in light years, gravity or flashes. Bloom as a white flower. I will claim both our innocence before we wither.'

Xan woke up and knew his grandmother had died and he wept.

He found her last note to him when he broke into her apartment and found her dead with the TV screen frozen on William Holden. He was embracing Nancy Kwan in a traditional dress that are now known in fashion simply by the actress's character name: Suzie Wong. In the note she asked him to strictly hang no portrait of her as she was old now and any picture of her when she was young and beautiful would be idiotic and that she should also be buried naked, as that is how she came into the world. That it should be her tank picture photograph on the old nail in the funeral hall. The picture changes at each death in the funeral hall but the nail never does, so this photo like the rusted nail was more honest. She was sorry she had asked him to do this but she could not trust anyone else to carry out her wishes. She wanted her epitaph to be the following. It was a part retelling of an old folk tale by an early 20th century writer, Lu Xun.

> *Yi threw back his head to hurl a curse at the sky. He watched and waited. But the moon paid no attention. He took three paces forward, and the moon fell back three paces. He took three paces back, and the moon moved forward. Yi, having killed every wild animal in and beyond his lands, lost his consort, who, bored with nothing but crow to eat, stole the elixir that allowed him to fly to the heavens and instead she chose to go to live by herself, alone on the moon.*

It was a contemporary retelling of one her special folk stories as a child and although she still had her doubts about Mao Zedung she knew Lu Xun was one of Mao's favourite writers and despite the sentiment of the epitaph she remained a hopeless romantic for Mao. After all, she wrote, 'We would rather sing the praises of another brick in the democratic wall than ever sing again the praises of a saviour like Mao.' But she understood why no one else would get that.

She wanted no name on her tombstone and no date, just this part from the story. The money to do all this was in her jar shaped like a tiger in the kitchen. She told him she knew he would find the archetype for the internet and that she had found hers and finally that he should dump Yi and get someone nice like Nancy Kwan, and that he should go to the Himalaya to find her. The money for that too was in the tiger jar.

Xan bought his ticket to Lhasa. He found a picture that Yi had emailed him of a Tibetan girl modelling by an exotic Italian sports car wearing expensive couture clothing in a modernised shopping mall in a 5 star hotel in Lhasa, Tibet. She was as far removed from the Tibetan girls he had imagined but not too far from the Hollywood fantasy of Suzie Wong. Yi was underwhelmed when Xan told her he was going away for a while and she said she would make do and matter of factly find someone else to date on the countless dating apps and maybe she would reconnect with some old boyfriends on WeChat. Xan knew, for his grandmother had told him, that philosophy was disappointment. So he remained stoic as the only two women he really knew, Yi and his grandmother, both spoke in the same blunt fashion. He figured at least he knew where he stood with them and with Yi that was not very far. Before he left she told him to download WISH. It sounded promising but then she told him it was the largest shopping mall on earth and that it was eBay crossed with Instagram. Yi told him that in the future—which was now—billions of smart things in the physical world will be sensing, responding, communicating and sharing data; it could generate its own power, its own electricity and both buy it and sell it; it could charge all our homes and manage our health. Cities and regions will never be the same again as everything will be disrupted. It will be an internet of everything. It will change money, business and the world. It will be a revolution.

> *A revolution is not a dinner party, or writing an essay, or painting a picture, or doing embroidery … so gentle, so temperate, so kind, courteous, restrained and magnanimous. A revolution is an uprising, an act of violence by which one class overthrows the power of the other.*
>
> —Mao Zedung (1927)

Xan texted that to Yi. Her one word reply was, 'Wateva.'

When Xan arrived in Lhasa, Tibet the first building he saw was a giant modern memorial that represented Mount Everest, a 37 metre high concrete white edifice, the Monument to the Peaceful Liberation of Tibet. He read a plaque declaring the expelling of imperialist forces by the People's Liberation Army, and he thought of his grandmother. He went to find his hotel located on the far east side of town. Again, the Intercontinental Lhasa Paradise was not quite what he expected: a collection of towering white polymer and smoked glass modernist pyramids emerged beside the ancient mountains. Xan was a child of modernity but in his heart and in his mind he felt out of time. He inhabited a state opposite to dejà vu, that of jamais vu or never seen. The whole world to him in all its seemingly solid modernist constructions and established narratives, be they economic, political or religious, was as if he was seeing them all for the very first time, like a time traveller or a man who had awoken from the ice after thousands of years of sleep, indeed just like the 5000 year old high altitude shepherd Otzi found by amongst others Reinhold Messner in the Alps, or like the 3000 year old Tarim mummy in the Xinjiang province of China from the desert basin beneath the Mountain of Heaven in the Tian Shan Mountain range, the Celestial Mountain range that links to the Himalaya. Xan had once driven the long Highway 291 that transversed the 3000 km mountain range from Xinjiang to Tibet, but he stopped short of Lhatse, Tibet—this was the highway his grandmother drove in Mao's armoured division of the People's Liberation Army. It was on this pass into Tibet she said she first felt the change that happened to her, that preceded her vision of the Yeti. She would tell him how she saluted the Kunlun Mountain Goddess, the highest mountain in the Kunlun Shan as she drove her tank in the armoured column, and it was here that she felt the energy of Hsi Wang Mu—Spirit Mother of the West, the great Queen Mother enter her. She would action the rumble of her tank and recite her oracle: '*In heaven, beneath heaven, in three worlds, and in the ten directions, all women who ascend to transcendence and attain the way are her dependents.'*

He went because his grandmother told him of the gravity of the oracle and that it was sacred even to a Marxist like her, but he went also to part hike one of the highest elevated volcanoes in the world at 19,000ft above sea level, the Kunlun Volcanic group, the only such volcanoes in the Chinese part of the vast Himalaya, itself another lost world, that had always enchanted him in its strangeness. But also his grandmother insisted he must visit these mountains, the Paradise of Taoism and the home of the Jade Palace of the legendary Yellow Emperor, before he visit Tibet.

Xan knew of all these discoveries and the legends of China and he was fascinated by them. Everything different in nature or in the distant past he felt more comfortable with, in many ways he felt able to navigate the past far more easily than the present, which he seemed to stumble through. Now he was struggling with finding the wifi password in the world's highest Intercontinental hotel in Lhasa, Tibet so that he could contact Yi online. As he sat in the luxury and warmth of what was a very fine room with chandeliers and decorated in a Louis XIV French fantasy of brocaded drapes and silk cushions and ornate gilded mirrors, it seemed although comfortable, strangely empty, as if it was a thin veneer, an impermanence that could dissolve. Or maybe it was because he was lonely thinking about his dead grandmother. He was thinking clearly now about Yi and that they had never met, except online, that she was maybe just a fembot or an avatar, that she was nothing like he imagined at all or indeed nothing at all—a complex algorithm responding to his questions with a collection of exported and exquisitely designed answers. In her last text message, Yi told him that the borders of the world, nation states and ideas of identity were to be no more. In the technological revolution of the internet of everything, what was China and what was Tibet or America or anywhere in Europe or elsewhere in Asia or any human populated island on earth would be dissolved. His grandmother said that he would find the archetype of the internet from an intermediate state or a dream.

He stared to look out to the vast Himalaya before him and thought about the Yeti she claimed to have seen on a high mountain pass. She was dead now, and he thought for a moment that maybe the Yeti was the living dead, a lost fragment of an ancient hominid, its numbers so few and now even more likely reduced to a mere handful, such that any population was unsustainable. So even if it was real at one point when his grandmother saw it in the 1950s, it was probably extinct by now. He held a longing that it was not, the 2,400 km range and the emptiness and the numerous places no humans had yet visited gave him hope that it might be hanging on. He respected this lost hairy cousin, the inhabitant of what was a lost Shangri La, a Shambhala, an Eden. It did not need a credit card, a car, clothes, a mobile phone, a supermarket, a tank, a vast shopping mall, a hotel, an ideology or a religion. Then he thought that it is we who are the real living dead in a zombie-like status lost in materialism, despite our progress, nothing learned and everything forgotten. He was in a poor state of mind but he was in grief, all despite laying upon a very opulent bed in a 5 star hotel courtesy of the money his grandmother left, but this only served to amplify his existential isolation. He was feeling very sorry for himself and hoping Yi could help him. He thought about her while he waited for his phone to ping an incoming text or WeChat message.

He thought about his dream and what exactly is the archetype of the internet? Computer code is written in binary, zeros and ones, he thought. The most successful technology and computer company is Apple. The individual who first came up with the idea of artificial memory and built a code breaking computation device or computer was Alan Turing, an Englishman during the war. He may have watched Black Narcissus, thought Xan. Xan knew that Turing committed suicide by eating a poisoned apple. The Tree of Knowledge in biblical creation tales contains an apple. The serpent tells the first woman Eve to make the first man Adam eat with her the apple. Binary with its zero is symbolically like an apple and the one symbolically like a serpent thought Xan. The internet is information, but information like never before, thought Xan. Like a tree with its vast growing fruit of information, a great apple of knowledge and computer information is in bytes. This information can be a good thing or it can be a bad thing, it depends, thought Xan. To pass the time Xan had been working on a disruptive hacking code on the flight from Chengdu to Lhasa. Before he left he went to Nanxing by the Yazi River, fed from the far Himalaya, to gaze upon the eye worshippers in the museum—a great lost civilisation with no written records and the most ancient in China, to look upon the mysterious colossal bronze smiling head with its protruding eyes on stalks as if captured in a perpetual state of jamais vu or a frozen moment of wonder of witnessing a Yeti perhaps, thought Xan. He realised he was fed up with much, his fellow youth constantly fixed to their Android devices and perceiving the world through a screen. He was fed up with his invisible girlfriend who lived her life entirely online. He was hoping his grandmother was right and he would find a new girlfriend at the roof of the world. Maybe it might be the beautiful Tibetan model Yi sent him? He was so utterly in despair that he wished to construct a disruptive self-repeating and evolving hacking code that would only leave a faint footprint of its first trail but then disappear from trace so it could not be found and resolved. He wanted to disrupt the revolution that Yi had predicted by using its own formula against it. As he sat in the hotel and gazed at the mountain range he was waiting for Yi to respond, as she would be the first victim of the contagion he would spread via email, text and app download with his new hack. He felt some satisfaction by sending Yi what would be his shortest message ever online. This he hoped would baffle her. Its one cryptic line just identified the four computing tech terms: Yobibyte Export Terminus I/o, by which his computer code, with its suicidal technology virus, would collapse the internet of everything. He felt some added satisfaction as he could never be traced as the source—as the ingenious contagion would only take place once he had inseminated her computer and it would be her response that would set fire to the technology just as the Tigers Nest was ablaze in his dream he thought. He imagined he was riding the pregnant tigress with Yi coming forth from the flames and the serpent whip she was wielding was the archetype of the internet. So he had simply sent Yi the single word: yobibytexporterminusi/o.

His mobile phone pinged, he read the response from Yi. She, whom or whatever Yi was, was pregnant with the contagion that he had inseminated in her devices, she had given birth in her response, and in doing so, had lit the match of his technological contagion. Her return message which would collapse the technological world was as usual shorter than his, but it also surprised him: she had identified the acronym for his conflation of Yobibyte Export Terminus I/o, it simply read: YETI.

EPILOGUE ONE

It is still a long way up, it's a long way down. Despite all the assisted oxygen, guides and modern equipment and NASA inspired hydrated foods, still the mountain claims lives in the hundreds; the harsh rock, ice and snow seriously injures many more, and the vast 2,400 km range of the mountains along with its attendant earthquakes that have helped form it, have a far greater death and injury list; but it is the many man-made wars in its past and that continue in the countries with their shifting borders and nationalist and tribal and religious conflicts that sit on its escarpments and land below that add to the vast toll and far surpass any natural disaster or 'accident'. The mountains and rocks and ice and snow and plateaus remain uninterested in our human affairs that barely skim its surface, even the odd nuclear test inside a bore-driven deep mine in the Kashmir, and the new tunnelling and road constructions and airports in a competitive frenzy being set up by the rival economic and military emergent powers China and India, were always thought by philosophers to remain insignificant. However, in this new age of the anthropocene that could be finally changing.

EPILOGUE TWO

Erik Weihenmayer is blind. He climbed further than the sighted can see when he reached the summit of Everest in May 2001. Some years later he was contacted by an excellent horse rider Sabriye Tenberken who is also blind with a suggestion that he assist her and six Tibetan children to climb the 23,000ft Lhakpa Ri in the shadow of Mount Everest. All the children were blind. The children were brought up in an orphanage created and ran by Sabriye for Tibetan children who were abandoned by their parents, scorned by the local populace and deemed unclean by some traditional devout Buddhists who see them as incarnated with a disability because they were sinners in a past life. Given none of the advantages and all of the disadvantages, they become street children and beggars in order to survive, open to all kinds of exploitation and cruelty. In Tibet blindness is a problem as some people feel the blind, even children, are possessed of demons. Tibet is a lot more complicated behind the fantasy and undeliverable projections of spiritual awakening and spiritual materialism that afflicts its westerner devotees. The great Himalaya are besieged by climbers and hikers as in the West it's important to be on top, to ascend the very summit. In the East it is not so. Sabriye tells the children the top is not important, it's more important that they are all together and they are having fun.

EPILOGUE THREE

George Mallory and Andrew Irvine were less than a kilometre from the summit of Everest in 1924. They lost their VPK camera—a vest pocket camera. It was long thought if found it would reveal if they were indeed the first humans to reach the summit.

A young Pakistani boy, Mohammed was himself lost in the vast Himalaya after trekking from Hunza into Tibet and down across and into Bhutan. In a shifting glacier at a lower reach of the Holy Mother he found an intact 1920s VPK camera. After he recovered he told his tale of buried Qurans and Taliban, snow leopards, distant cities and Tin in Tibet. But he told no one of the camera he found. Then a year or so later with a dark-room specialist he found a way to develop its contents. Out of the dim red light a faded black and white image of two period-dressed climbers appeared, other images at varying altitudes, both at the summit and on their descent, then two shots of strange oversize footprints in snow and ice, and then one last shot of what looked like the arm of a hairy bear. It was difficult to make out if this was a hairy paw or a hairy hand holding the mountaineer's ration tin? Mohammed did not wait, instead he ran into the street jumping, shouting in all the languages he knew, 'I Mohammed went to the mountain. I found the Yeti, I found the Yeti with Tin in Tibet.'

The Yeti is not like us
and it does not like us. The Yeti
cannot be like you
but, you might, one day,
if you are inside the Yeti
be like the Yeti,
but not Yeti. The Yeti might
leave a trail for you,
a track, or an object,
or an arrangement
Or you may glimpse the shade of the Yeti
feel its presence
If you are blessed
Some mourn and grieve for the Yeti and confess
Even if they are mocked
that they dreamt the Yeti
They venerate the Yeti

This is a noble path

www.ingramcontent.com/pod-product-compliance
Lightning Source LLC
Chambersburg PA
CBHW041754010726
47507CB00009B/389

* 9 7 8 1 9 1 1 5 9 7 0 7 0 *